I DO (NO'T)

ABOVE THE LAW

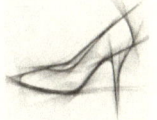

ALICE VL

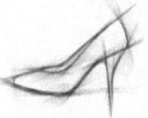

Copyright 2018

I DO (NOT)

Part 4

ABOVE THE LAW

Alice VL

I DO (NOT) – ABOVE THE LAW

Alice VL

BRAVO, TEN FOUR!

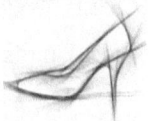

Ally Bradshaw saying Bravo, *Ten Four*!

Whatever. My luck was bound to run out, *not that it was any good to begin with*, and everything was bound to coming crashing down around me sooner or later. I just thought it would be later, *rather* than sooner. I certainly did not think it would be at the hands of this rough guy, Detective Rough!

My little escapade with the detective begins at the precinct minutes after I get back from Water Hills where Daniel, Lucy *woozy* and I meet with him following the fire at the museum and which prompted my sudden and surprisingly unwilling return to Willow County. Yes, *unwilling*.

As you know, I was instantly and unashamedly bowled over by his bad-ass'*ness,* his rough boy looks and oh so smooth talk.

Naturally, I am a little intimidated by Mark as we begin *detectiving* through the case – *together*. Yes, detectiving. I *know*, I need to ask for my school fees back. Daniel is still shacking up with the perfect porcelain princess, and to be honest, I am waiting for that bubble to burst. *I don't like her,* and I have a feeling, I'm going to like her even less as she continues to cling to Daniel like a perfect little damsel in distress.

A run-in with Michael leads to an unexpected, but all the same, *unfair* calamity, and when Mark sets his sights on that pathetic ex-husband of mine, I actually feel sorry for him as he becomes a target in more investigation than one. Lily too. I'm not sure how I feel about *that?*

Speaking of Michael; he's proposed to Lily and they couldn't be happier. *Whoop. Whoop. I* can't be happier.

Anyway, back to this rough boy detective, things are not quite as they seem and even though the sensual side of me refuses to quite see what my mind sees, I find myself in a little bit of a legal wrangle and an unlawful mess.

My encounter with Mark turns into a scene from an action-packed-thriller starring *me* (who else?), Michael, Lily and Daniel. How was I to know that *that* detective thought himself above the law? Yes, I know what I *hoped* for, but not like *that?*

Hold on tight; this is one adventure I never want to repeat. This is one time I kinda' wished that I was still that boring, drab and ugly *wifey.* This scared the shit out of me and almost numbed and locked my passionate alter ego up *forever,* and possibly beyond.

But, it's also made me realize quite a few things about myself, and how far I would go to defend the innocent, whether I like them or *not*. It made me see a side of Michael I had forgotten still existed, but also a side to Daniel that perhaps I just never *wanted* to see before.

Whatever. I am looking at life a little differently lately, and when all is said and done, I still have a heart. Feelings. Emotions. Fears. Needs. Desires. *Wants*.

Wants. Maybe I've missed a moment that I might come to regret for the rest of my life, but maybe, the fat lady hasn't yet sung? *Who knows?*

What I do know is that Michael has seen better days, and that Daniel is *living* better days. Me? I'm still reeling from all that went down with Detective Mark Warren. You can definitely not call me boring or drab, possibly ugly, but *don't*. It stings.

Ally!

Alice VL

I DO (NOT) – ABOVE THE LAW

PART 1

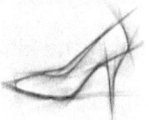

Detective Mark *'Hotness'* Warren led us through a long, dark corridor, away from the noise of the precinct and into what appeared to be an interrogation room.

It was cold, dark and interrogatory. *'Oh Lawd, Ally. Interrogatory?'* These men are really no good for my knowledge of the English language, or the education my parents' had paid for with their blood, sweat and tears. I was a rule-follower, I still am *sort of*, and making words up as I go is undeniably an insult to my education. I am pretty sure I'll come around the moment the trampy side of me gets with the program. *Fingers crossed!*

It was intimidating and spooky and for a moment, every single little thing I had ever done wrong in my life, began to flash right before my eyes. I could not imagine sitting in there and being on the wrong side of the law. *'Yikes.'*

Daniel and I followed him inside, but not before he asked, or rather, insisted that Lucy wait for us in an even more depressing waiting area. *'Take that bitch.'* I couldn't help but wonder how many fathers had waited for their sons in there, or how many mothers were waiting to identify their children's bodies. It was dispiriting to say the least. The very idea sent shivers down my spine, and not the kind of shivers you and I both know I'd rather be discussing.

Almost like a prison cell, a bulb hung from the ceiling lighting up the room just enough to cast a light on plastic chairs around a table.

Daniel and I sat down at a wooden table in the center of the room before Detective Warren took a seat across from us. When he glanced over at a camera in the corner of the room, I knew at once that he was wholly acquainted with the antics of interrogation; something he must have done a thousand times before.

"So, Miss Bradshaw ... do you have any idea who would want to set fire to the museum?"

I frowned and tried to think of *any* one person that might have walked into the museum that seemed oddly out of place, or someone I, or my staff might have had a run-in with, or even someone who simply came in looking for employment.

In all honesty, I didn't know *anyone* at all who would deliberately set fire to the museum, or would feel that they were wronged by the museum staff in any way. Not by me personally, and certainly not by the museum. It absolutely wasn't an act of retaliation or revenge.

"I don't …"

Daniel leaned forward and placed his elbow on the table,

"We responded to a fire right next door to the museum a few months before this incident. The modes operandi seems eerily similar, almost identical, and we have reason to believe it might be a local gang. Word on the street a while ago was that it was a spade of initiations, but how far that is true, I can't tell you?"

Mark Warren nodded his head and quickly scribbled a few words onto a notepad in front of him. When he looked back at me, my heart just about thumped right from my chest. He looked like a swimwear, or underwear model, but rugged and without charm. He came across as uptight and rigid, and when he spoke, I would guess that he was ex-military.

His dark hair was slightly too short, and his eyes weren't really heart-stopping, but there was a look in them I just couldn't ignore. I couldn't put a finger on it, but there was something there that drew me to him like a magnet.

Alice VL

I DO (NOT) – ABOVE THE LAW

They were a deep, earthy brown but there was something else in them. I thought of an old copper penny that is held against powerful flames, reflecting a sort of brownish, yellowish light. When he looked over at Daniel, it was as though cinnamon was swirling in his eyes.

"We must consider all possibilities. We are well-acquainted with the fire of a few months back, but it's important to either connect these fires or to treat it as an unrelated case. We can't just assume that they were all caused by one person or one group."

I glowered questioningly at him.

'What other possibilities could there be?'

"Do you have an ex-boyfriend, husband or rejected lover who might be angry enough to do this?"

I was stunned. *'No. Of course not.'* I glanced over at Daniel who had begun scowling at Detective Warren. When he turned to me, his mouth was pursed but slightly open. His eyes were fixed on me as though he was waiting for me to rubbish Detective Warren's assumptions as ridiculous. *Which they were.*

I DO (NOT) – ABOVE THE LAW

"No, not at all. I mean, I am divorced but … Michael, my ex-husband, would never do that. He's happy and has moved on … he holds no grudges …"

'Has he?' I felt no need to inform Detective Warren of the events that unfolded only recently. I didn't want to tell him how low Ally Bradshaw stooped by exacting revenge on my cheating, scumbag ex-husband. There was no way in the world that Michael would go as far as to set fire to the museum. After all, he had already attainedrevenge by bitterly complaining to my parents. Detective Warren quickly jotted down something else, before he closed his notepad. I had to make a concerted effort to ignore Daniel's sharp gaze, as though to nudge me about my incident with Michael. I didn't want to lay it all out in front of the detective while knowing that Michael who had many questionable flaws, was not an arsonist.

"Alright. I think I have what I need. If you could just leave me your contact details, I'll let you know the moment there is any news. We are waiting for the Willow County Fire Department, which is you Daniel, to release your findings. Once we have that, we have something to go on."

"Alright." Daniel nodded and shook Mark's hand.

Alice VL

I DO (NOT) – ABOVE THE LAW

Mark Warren slid a blank sheet of paper over to me and placed a pen next to it. I could feel him stare at me and was slightly bewildered. I didn't think it was an intentionally cold stare, but somehow, his face lacked the mobility he usually had.

I was uncomfortable and when I looked back at him, it was almost as though there was no life behind his eyes. I instantly felt as though I was the enemy while staring into what sent shivers down my spine. His eyes were cold and hard. I took in a deep breath when at once, the burning stare he gave me was suddenly gone. With every move his eyes made on me after the unnerving stare of only moments ago, his intentions were betrayed, and there was not one thing noble about them. I was bordering on fear for him, but flattered all at the same time.

After jotting down my number, I quickly slid the sheet back to him. I glanced over at Daniel who I was sure, had become unintentionally irritated.

'What is he seeing?' When Detective Warren got up from his chair, Daniel and I both stood up. *'Is that it?'*

"Thank you, Detective Warren. I appreciate your help."

I shook his hand and was once again highly seduced by his strong grip. Daniel again offered him an extended hand when I let go and shook it vigorously.

Alice VL

I DO (NOT) – ABOVE THE LAW

"Thanks for seeing us, Mark. I, as does Ally, appreciate your time."

"You're welcome buddy. Be safe out there."

"Thanks."

Daniel placed his arm on my back, and led me out of that cold, nasty interrogation room. I was at once highly distracted by his intoxicating, seducing, over-powering and seductive scent. *Again.* I suspected at once that Daniel Sotherby was going to be the death of me. When we reached the waiting area, Daniel held a hand out to Lucy before he turned around to face me,

"I hope they catch these guys ..."

I nodded. I hoped so too. The museum was my sanity, my back-to-reality, my real world.

"Yep ... I hope so too."

Lucy *poppy-woozy* stood up and immediately took his hand before she oh so lovingly leaned against him. I truly, into the very core of my being and existence, *didn't* like that girl. The expression on her face was one of triumph when she flicked her long blonde hair to one side and smiled victoriously at me.

Let's face it, I am hardly any competition for girls like Lucy. By clinging to him and simpering softly, she basically won hands-down. The way she giggled each time Daniel said anything, funny or not, she giggled and there is nothing I could say or do to show my irritation.

Daniel's friendship was important to me and to be honest, I am ordinary and will never compete with a woman whose life is directed by way of fashion magazines, manicured nails and overly made-up eyes.

"Bye Ally ... oh and good to have you home again."

Daniel smiled before they both turned away from me.

"Bye Daniel, thanks."

He waved cautiously when he turned back to me again. I waited a second longer before I walked out behind them. He had placed his arm around Lucy's waist and held her tightly against him as they made their way back to his truck, like any normal, committed and loving couple. *Couple*. I had a strange feeling that each time I would run into Lucy-*woozy*, I'd let myself hate her even though she probably in no way at all, deserves to be despised.

When I reached my car, I shifted into the driver's seat, and stared at them. *Them*. How could Daniel become one half of a them, just like that? It was undeniably clear that he had a high opinion of her; I just didn't expect that he would fall for her, or anyone for that matter, and so soon.

When they finally pulled out of the parking, I was at once aware of sharp sting deep inside of me somewhere. It was my own fault and my own doing. I pulled him closer with one hand and pushed him away with another. I knew *that* about me but I just couldn't stop doing that. Was I perhaps manipulating my emotions to disguise the way I truly felt about Daniel, and what was I feeling for him?

Why Daniel had such immense power over me, I would probably never know. I didn't like the way I felt when I saw him with Lucy, but *still*, I knew very little of what I want. I honestly, truly and into the depths of me, didn't know what I wanted.

What I did know was that I had just met and have been somewhat swept off my feet by Detective Warren at the precinct, and I was secretly hoping that he would use my number for something other than keeping me in the loop with his hunt for these arsonists. So instead of analyzing my feelings for Daniel, I kept my fingers crossed that Mark Warren might be what I needed to snap out of whatever I had fallen into with the fireman.

I DO (NOT) – ABOVE THE LAW

I took my mobile from my bag, and hurriedly dialed Bianca. I hadn't spoken to her in a week, and I doubted she even knew that I was back in Willow County.

Bianca, as usual, answered after the very first ring.

"Ally Wally?

"Hello beautiful … are you home?"

"You're back?"

"Yep … long story."

"I'm always home … come on, I'll chill the wine."

Bianca religiously and in the nick of time, snapped me out of any mood I would find myself in, effortlessly. I was happy to be back; happy to have seen Daniel again but even more so, I was excited to catch up with Bianca and tell her all about the events that unfolded in Water Hills, and let's not forget Ryan *Cowboy* Henderson.

When I reached Bianca's cottage a short while later, I pulled up into her driveway, but before I could climb out my car, my mobile phone began bleeping frantically. The messages were coming through in quick succession of each other, all from Daniel.

"Sorry about Lucy."

Alice VL

"Nice to see you."

"You look good."

"Welcome home."

"I missed you."

The walloping in my heart was undeniable when I read each message. On point always, Daniel knew what to say, when to say it and how to make me feel like the most important woman in the world. He still knew how to make me his queen, even though it was only in *my* mind.

"Thanks Danny. I missed you more." I *did* miss him and I wanted him to know that.

When I finally climbed out my car, Bianca could hardly contain her animation, and when I reached her front door, she flung her arms around me.

"One week. You lasted one week with your parents!"

She was right, of course, but not for the reasons she was thinking of. *At all.*

"I know! But, seriously, I *didn't* want to come back."

Alice VL

Bianca stopped walking and turned back to me. The expression on her face was priceless when she frowned and glared at me without as much as blinking.

"I'll tell you all about it, and if it wasn't for the fire at the museum, I'd still be there … but then again, I probably wouldn't have met Detective Mark Warren."

"Oh God, Ally. I can't keep up with you! You actually had fun back home? You've been back all of five minutes and throwing out names like detective who?"

"Don't judge me."

We walked inside and when Bianca shut the front door behind me, I quickly made my way over to her dining room table. She hurriedly poured us each a glass of wine, before she slipped into a chair across from me.

"So?"

"Aah Bianca. I had a fabulous time in Water Hills. I was so nervous on my drive there, but then I met a gorgeous cowboy on the first night of the Annual Fall Festival. We just clicked and hit it off straight away."

"Now, how did I know that would happen?"

I DO (NOT) – ABOVE THE LAW

"My parents were a little tight and stiff the first few days. I think I've told you that they're still having a hard time with Max's death?"

"Yep ... I feel badly for you guys."

"Well, my mom found a letter Max wrote her when he was around twelve or thirteen and she just sort of snapped out of her grief. Like instantly."

"Wow. Max wrote her a letter?"

"Yep. But, then shit happened. As you might have guessed by now, it follows me. Heather, my brother's ex-girlfriend's *best* friend, Georgia has had her eye on Ryan forever, and recorded us doing the dirty in the stables. She then went on and played it on the big screen on movie night and in front of just about the entire Water Hills community. It was *awful*."

"She recorded you doing it?'

I nodded. My face had turned bright red just thinking of the scene that played out on the big screen. I cringed, and just couldn't get the images of us on display for all to see, off my mind.

"Oh my word! Your parents must have lost their shit."

I placed my glass of wine down and smiled,

Alice VL

I DO (NOT) – ABOVE THE LAW

"You should have seen my parents. They jumped into action and took my side. My mom didn't hesitate, neither did my dad. I wish you were there Bianca. She socked it to the whole Water Hills that night."

Bianca almost choked on her wine,

"You're shitting me?"

I giggled and picked up my glass of wine.

"It was great. My mother stood there exposing the secrets of the entire holier than though folks of Water Hills."

"So, no preacher, no Michael shit?"

"Nope, not a single word. Like I said, it was an issue in the beginning, but my parents just left it there."

Bianca was stunned and I, in retrospect, was still a little dumbfounded by my mother's unanticipated, yet heroic behavior.

"I just saw Daniel though. He met me at the precinct."

"Oh?"

"Yep, he responded to the fire at the museum and wanted to meet me there before he hands in his report to

Detective Warren. The detective wanted to know if I knew of anyone that might deliberately have set fire to the museum."

"How did it feel to see him again?"

"My heart fluttered. There were butterflies as usual."

"I told you, Ally Bradshaw ... you're falling for him."

"I'm *not*. Besides, he's dating a blonde bimbo, Lucy *woozy* something."

"You are such a bitch Ally, what if she's really nice?"

"She's not."

We sat around the dining room table for another hour or so, and when I glanced at my wrist watch, I did not expect it to be as late as it was. I instantly berated myself for not letting my father know I had arrived safely. I quickly texted my parents and was sure that at any minute, my dad would be calling the entire Willow County, convinced that I was lying in a ditch somewhere after crashing my car.

When my dad responded, I swiftly gulped down the last of my wine, and made the short trip back to my apartment. As much as I didn't want to leave Water Hills, I was happy to be home and back in my apartment. I still had two weeks of holiday leave left, and I was looking forward to spending time at Helen's, and of course, spending more time with Bianca.

The plan for the next couple of days was to relax by watching movies, and shopping for winter's clothes. Fall was in full swing, but it might as well have been winter. The nights and early mornings were getting colder, even though the days warmed up quite drastically.

After unpacking my suitcases, and making myself a cup of coffee, I turned on the taps and sat on the edge of the tub. I took my mobile phone and quickly messaged Daniel,

"I *did* miss you."

I wanted him to know. I *did* miss him. I thought of him often and being back home in Water Hills hardly changed any of that. Ryan was an amazing and noble guy. He was attractive and the owner of a magnificent scent that took me on rides I could never have imagined to be taken on.

With all that said, I was pretty sure it was Daniel the *fireman*, I wanted to come home to. He was home to my heart.

'No, he isn't.'

I just wanted to be close to him. *'Ally Bradshaw, zip it.'* I was engaged in a constant warfare with my emotions where my heart and my mind didn't agree on any point at all, and instead, were engaged in combat and constant conflict. *'Urgh.'* Who wins? Who knows? As strong as my heart was, as fearless was my mind.

When I climbed into the bath, I involuntarily closed my eyes. I was exhausted and laid reflecting on the past week. I thought of Detective Warren and was intrigued by him. I couldn't help but wonder if his tough, strong and overbearing appearance was perhaps, just a facade. I *sort of* liked that about him.

My imagination was once again running around wild in my head as I fantasized about him bursting through my front door and placing me under immediate arrest. Once under arrest, I wanted him to punish me and sentence me to at least a few weeks of hard time. Hard, rigid and unyielding-time. A sensual kind of sentence as I served a confined term of cuffs, ties and blindfolds. *'Oh Lord, Ally.'*

I honestly couldn't decide where those thoughts were coming from or how they found their way into my mind. I was not *that* kind of girl, I wasn't, but damn, I was surrounded by beasts of flavors and sorts, and I couldn't be happier.

When I finally climbed out the bath, I threw my robe over me and glared at my reflection in the mirror. When I noticed that my once beautiful auburn locks were just about lost underneath the re-growth of my dark hair, I quickly dialed Helen.

"Helen speaking."

"It's me, Ally. Sorry to worry you so late."

"No worries. What's up?"

"Have you got any time for me tomorrow?"

"Sure. The same?"

"Yep, hair and wax."

"No problem. Around noon?"

"Perfect. Thanks Helen."

"See you tomorrow!"

When I ended my call to Helen, I noticed a new text message from Daniel,

"Good."

'Good? That's it? Good?'

I was convinced that Lucy must have been messing with his mind, but more than that, I was offended that she had taken control of a certain power over Daniel. *'Good?'* I did not like his response, and when I climbed into bed, all I could think of was how he was sharing himself with her. I was horrified and felt a sudden sting jab at me when I considered his arms wrapped around her, or that her nails were carving into him.

I didn't want his scent to sweep her off her feet. *It was mine.* The idea of his mouth around hers, or his lips pressed against hers, or his hands carved into her was enough to make my head spin. It nauseated me.

'I can't think of that. I can't think like that.' I knew that it would drive me insane. *'Ally Bradshaw, you are your own worst enemy.'*

I lifted the covers over my head and forced Daniel and Lucy from my mind. My thoughts drifted back to Ryan and the events of the past week. I reflected on Georgia, and wondered if that country girl could ever imagine what she was getting and whether she would appreciate and wholly absorb Ryan's sensuality like I did.

'Lucky girl.'

Alice VL

Helen's place was buzzing when I walked in just before noon the following day. I didn't usually *like* sitting between dozens other women who I might say, make me feel just a tad bit lesser and drab.

With their whispers and fake smiles, I looked for signs on their cheeks that would expose their forced smiles all day long. They were the kind of women that could grace any billboard or magazine cover. They were beautiful without the necessity of three-dimensional photo shopping that models set the tone for and that we try so hard to imitate and set our own standards by.

They would come in in tailored suits with their feet up on Helen's couches as their toe nails were primed and painted. They were of the glamorous sorts who might as well be getting ready for the red carpet.

These were the women that loved to hate other women. Movie star good looks, tall and willowy. Most were blessed with flawless bone structures and silk-like skin.

Then there was me, *Ally*. A plain Jane. Simple. Curly hair that often, couldn't tell the difference between curls and waves. I am so pale that even in the dark you could see me shining like a beacon. But, I am confident and *nice*.

Alice VL

I DO (NOT) – ABOVE THE LAW

When Helen spotted me trying to sneak in unnoticed, she quickly showed me to the wash basin, and before I could tell her that I didn't mind waiting in a corner somewhere, my hair was washed, and the color applied.

"So, how are you darling?"

"I'm good thanks."

"How's that fireman you were going so on about?"

"Uhm …"

"It's over already?"

"Well, no. We're friends. I've since met a Doctor Walker and a cowboy."

"Ally Bradshaw!"

"I know. I am such a bad person."

"So, which one is it now?"

My phone rang entirely out of the blue, interrupting and saving me from what would most certainly turn into an uncomfortable conversation with Helen,

"Ally Bradshaw."

"Miss Bradshaw, Detective Mark Warren …"

Alice VL

Wait for it. There it was; my foot instinctively began swinging from side to side.

"Hello detective …"

I swooned. *Just a little.* My reflection in the mirror confirmed a grin from ear to ear.

"I just wanted to keep you updated. We've received a tip-off that a suspected arson gang will be at a club tonight. I'll be going down there to see what I can find out."

"Oh, alright. Thank you."

"Nobody really knows what they look like, and I was hoping that you could meet me there. You might just have seen one of them before, or you might just recognize someone."

'Now that's more like it.'

"I would love to. I mean, if it *helps*?"

My heart raced frantically at the idea of meeting up with that rough-boy detective later that night.

'I have nothing to wear! Gosh Ally, you sound like these golden women around you.'

"Around ten? I'll meet you at Club Zero, in the private lounge? Do you know where it is?"

Alice VL

"Yes. Perfect. I'll be there."

Helen too, was beaming from ear to ear when I placed the mobile phone back in my purse. She made no attempt to hide the fact that she was eaves-dropping on my conversation with Detective Mark Warren.

"Which one is *he*?"

"He's the detective working on the arson case at the museum. It's just work."

"Uh huh?"

"Oh ssshh. Just make me beautiful ..."

Helen and I both burst out laughing. Who was I kidding? Work? *Whatever.*

It was a warm day, but the nights were colder, so I stopped off at Laurel's Boutique and picked up a beautiful tailored, long-sleeved evening dress.

It was not too shiny or glittery, but trashy enough in an elegant and classy way. Michael and I were never much for the night life, so needless to say, my wardrobe in that department was lacking.

Alice VL

I DO (NOT) – ABOVE THE LAW

I found a beautiful pair of six-inch heels to match a striking turquoise, rather low-cut dress. With my hair newly colored and flaming red, the rest of me was equally tailored and shiny. I was pretty sure I could pull off an evening knocking Detective Warren off his feet.

Alice VL

I DO (NOT) – ABOVE THE LAW

I pulled up in front of Club Zero just after ten that evening. There was a long line going down the block and when I considered walking to the very end of the line, I became a little flustered and anxious. *'I'll be in line for hours.'* I felt out of place, old and definitely not the type of person to be there. Nervously, I glanced around me and wondered who I was trying to fool. I didn't want to be there.

'Maybe, this isn't for me. Maybe, I should just start acting my age and be the lady I thought I was.' I considered texting Detective Warren, but when I realized that he would probably be there already, I found myself in a sudden frenzy.

'I'm leaving. I'll call him tomorrow.'

I was just about to start my car, when there was a sudden knock on my window, giving me the damn fright of my life, but to my instant relief, I recognized Detective Warren. He opened my door and made way for me to climb out.

"Hi."

"Wow. You look … just wow."

'Is there anything better than a reaction like this? Not in a thousand years.'

"You look nice too …"

Alice VL

'Nice?' He was striking in his faded jeans, buttoned shirt and wind-breaker. I scrutinized him from top to bottom and couldn't help but imagine *that* bad boy having his way with me.

"Were you going to leave?"

"Have you seen that line? I stuttered not knowing what to say to him.

"Come on ... let me show you how it's done."

'Ooh, I like that.' I could manage nothing more than a smile and a nod. *That's it.* I was speechless. Mark took my hand and walked slightly ahead of me.

When we reached the entrance to Club Zero, we were let in at once. The bodyguard, or bouncer, or whatever they are called these days was an extraordinarily big guy. Tall. *Bulky.* Mean-looking. Scary.

He was overpowering and intimidating with not a single expression on his face. When he recognized Detective Warren, he immediately greeted him by name and made way for us to enter without delay. I felt important. *Special.* Beautiful.

Detective Warren led me into what I assumed was a private lounge, and when we sat down on a leather couch, he quickly summoned a waiter. Around us were hundreds of conversations in equally loud voices, almost as though they were competing with the music in the background. The crowd was young, energetic and dominated the ambiance. It was definitely not my scene and when I noticed a young girl with heavily made up eyes crying in a corner at the bar, I became uncomfortable at once.

"What's your poison?"

'*Poison? You … right now.*'

"Wine … red."

"Bring us a bottle of Chardonnay."

'*Nice.*' He handed the waiter a large bill, before he turned back to me.

"So, keep an eye out. Apparently, this is *the* thug hang-out."

"This place? It's so busy and the vibe is so young; I can't imagine low-life thugs hanging out here?"

"Yeah well, that is exactly why they hang out here. We've heard rumors of them using this place to deal drugs, but we've never been able to verify any of it, or even catch them in the act here."

"Oh right."

'So, how are teenagers always finding these drug dealers, but the FBI, SWAT teams or special forces can't? Just a thought.'

"Try and blend in. I'd hate for you to stick out like a sore thumb."

"Do I?"

He moved closer to me and placed his arm around me. From his unkempt, dark hair peeked eyes that were a mix of hazel, honey and a little hint of olive. There was a certain unresponsiveness to them and I could only imagine it might have been as a result of years of witnessing events that no man should ever see.

There were the usual creases around them, but there was something else I again, could not quite place my finger on. Somewhere in those shadowy pools was an expression that was untaught to me. There was nothing warm, lively or even a hint of a sparkle in this man's eyes.

"Pretend you are the entertainment. A good time girl."

"Like ... a whore?"

"No, not like a whore."

He burst out laughing before he took my hand into his.

"A dancer … you certainly could pass for one of those exotic, sensual dancers."

I wasn't sure if I should have been flattered, or insulted? But, oh Lord, that would certainly not be a problem. When our wine was brought to the table, Mark quickly poured us each a glass, and lifted his to mine.

"Here's to you … and here's to me."

'Is he flirting with me or is this still pretend?'

"Here's to detectiving, Detective."

"Ally, call me Mark. Undercover, remember?"

"Right."

I rather liked calling him detective. It was intensely imposing, authoritative and commanding. My wine glass was filled to the brim, but I needed to loosen up, so I gulped down the entire glass. My nerves were failing me. Not only was I undercover, but I wanted so badly to get under *his* covers.

A group of young men, four or five I guessed to be in their early twenties walked in and sat on a corner couch crossways from us. Mark's face changed at once when, when what I

Alice VL

assumed to be the leader of the group, stopped and turned to us. Mark immediately lowered his head, anxious to conceal his identity.

The assumed leader was resting against a wooden pillar while gazing over at us as though he was waiting at a bus stop for a bus to pull in. He wasn't slumping; his muscular body didn't seem to allow for it. I didn't want to lock eyes with him but could barely turn away as I trailed over the ink covering his arms. I glanced over into his eyes and beneath his pierced brows, his eyes were firmly fixed on mine. He did not blink, even for a second.

'What do I do now?'

What was a girl to do? Slowly, like a seasoned undercover officer, I seductively slid onto Mark's lap, my back facing him. While arching my back in true working-girl style, I engaged in a lap dance while keeping an eye on the gangster man.

As though it was the only way my body truly knew how to speak, my sensuality began infecting my entire body. My limbs were suddenly like liquid in perfect rhythm with the music, surprising and flabbergasting myself all at the same time.

With what I hoped was dazzling grace that would take Mark's breath away, I unleashed emotions that moved with purposeful clarity. I was swept up in the moment, caught between convincing a thug surveying us, that I was nothing more than a party girl, and seducing Mark Warren all at the same time.

I peeked over at Mr. Gangster through the hair that had begun covering my face. He did nothing but grin before he turned to join the already seated group across from us. I peered over at them and snuck in a glimpse. I was horrified to notice that they had an unobstructed view of us and were peeking over every so often, almost as though they were making turns to watch what must have come across as a late-night tease show.

I knew then that I would have to engage in quite a bit more 'under covering' if I was to keep our cover guarded and safe. *Under covering*? What was becoming of my otherwise intelligent self?

Mark slid his arms around me as I moved slowly, still diligently committed to performing a sensual lap dance. Or rather, as sensually as I possibly *could*. His hands firmly gripped my hips as I conscientiously and meticulously teased him.

He slowly but assertively lowered his hands until they reached my thighs. I leaned forward slightly, desperate to conceal the trail his hands were following, from innocent spectators and especially, the gang in front of us.

Alice VL

I DO (NOT) – ABOVE THE LAW

Below me, I felt him press me onto him, and was no longer paying attention to the group in front of me. I no longer looked up when someone walked by, instead, I was caught up in the movements and shifting underneath me that my entire being was beginning to hunt.

His hands glided in underneath my dress and slowly tracked down until my breaths began to rise in almost visible puffs. At that very moment, I questioned whether I might have been a little too old for the scene playing out around me, and whether it should really have been all about silk sheets and rose petals. Still, in that moment I didn't really care and abandoned all thoughts of appropriateness.

His hands gently teased me as he hovered over my thighs with what felt like a raw intensity. I lowered my head, desperate to disguise the expression on my face. Thankfully, the deafening music was muffling my sounds, as Mark began shifting dangerously below me.

He suddenly reclaimed his hand when I moved slightly forward, allowing him to unzip his jeans. With his one hand firmly holding onto my thigh, the other clasping at my hips, I lifted a few inches more before he me pressed me back down onto him.

Alice VL

I DO (NOT) – ABOVE THE LAW

My eyes spontaneously closed before my head fell impulsively backwards, and my body began to move radically to the beat of the piercing music around us. Mark was still. He sat motionlessly as he held onto my hips with all his might.

I wasn't sure if it was the fear of getting caught, or the adrenalin that had begun rushing through me; I was not even sure if it was the idea of hanky-*pankying* in public, but within seconds, my entire body was overcome with ripples that turned to crashing waves without warning.

Yet, it wasn't as intense as I had grown acquainted to in the last few weeks. It was restricted, confined and contained. There was no intense quivering, thrills or shrills. There was no build up or slow warnings of what was to come.

From the moment he pressed himself against me, there was an immediate but subtle responsiveness to him and a quick, easy and mild sensation struck instantly. There was no summit ahead of me, no top to climb and no peak to reach. It was just *there*. Then it *wasn't*. The second-long high submerged me into the lowest of lows when it was over. Almost disappointing, yet intense all at once.

Alice VL

His powerful grip lessened almost all together, and when I lifted slightly off of him, he quickly pulled back, zipped up his jeans and pulled me back against him.

"Are they still looking?"

Without making it too obvious, I peered over at the group across from us and was instantly relieved that they showed no attentiveness to us.

"No."

I slid off Mark and huddled closely against him on the couch. I looked up at him, mortified by what we had just done in full view of the club. The adrenaline was still surging through my veins feeling as though my heart was about to explode and all I wanted to do was run for the hills. Instead, I remained right where I was.

There was nothing on Mark's face to betray any fear he might have had, instead, his expression was one of defiance and surety; as though *he* was the leader. As hard as I searched his face, there was no trace or evidence of what had just happened between us; no color change in his cheeks to betray him. From the corner of his eye, a muscle twitched involuntarily as he stared out at Mr. Gangster across from us before he turned back to me.

Alice VL

I DO (NOT) – ABOVE THE LAW

Mark frowned and almost as though he could read my mind, he took my hand and squeezed it,

"It's dark. We're in a corner. Nobody saw a thing, I promise."

I was instantly relieved and when I glanced around me, there was nothing that would make me think otherwise. Club Zero was filled with clubbers who were paying very little attention to much of anything around them.

As though high on a double dose of Ecstasy, I could have sworn that they were all dancing to what seemed like the Northern Lights with smoke filling the air in colors of blue, green and a hundred different shades of pink. The music was loud. *Deafening*. Clubbers' arms were waving from side to side, while heads were swaying, their eyes fixed on the floor below them.

Watching them move to the beat of the music below the crazy, blinding lights made me feel unexpectedly and surprisingly animated. Everyone around me was hyped-up and focused on themselves, ready for a good time. Why was I not?

I smiled. I was relieved. '*This is not me.*' This was not who Ally Bradshaw was. Nonetheless, I felt like such a bad-ass. Not proud. But *still*, a bad ass.

Alice VL

"Ally?"

'Oh Lord. Michael? Really?'

I turned and looked up to find Michael and Lily passing us, but when Michael recognized me, it stopped him dead in his tracks. I must be honest, the look on his face was priceless as he stood staring at me. But, in true Michael-style, he couldn't just pass us by and pretend he didn't see me. *No.* He just *had* to make his presence known.

"Michael ... you again?"

"What are you doing here?"

As though I had set foot on forbidden land, Michael seemed just a tad bit irritated by my presence.

'At. A. Night. Club.'

Mark stood up and glared dubiously at Michael,

"Mark Warren. Detective."

Michael turned to Mark, refused his extended hand, and turned back to me. My first thought was how accustomed he had become to being ill-mannered and disrespectful while feebly trying to hide what I recognized as jealousy.

Alice VL

I DO (NOT) – ABOVE THE LAW

'He must be the most offensive and discourteous man I have ever come across. How did I do this for twelve years?'

"I am here … doing what people do when they go to clubs. What are you doing here? I don't think I've ever seen you in a night club before?"

"Lily's bachelorette and my bachelor's is here … tonight."

Michael looked as though the world was weighing heavily on him. Lily wasn't looking too well either, and I could only assume that *he* was taking a toll on her.

"Oh?"

'Michael's proposed to Lily?'

"Congratulations! You two certainly deserve one another and I don't mean that in a bad way …"

I stood up and turned to Mark. The news was unexpected, and not that I cared, but the ink was hardly dry on our divorce papers.

"Mark, this is Michael, my *ex*-husband."

Mark sat down, and pulled me down with him before he took my hand into his,

"Well, is that a fact? All I can say is, thanks buddy."

Alice VL

Michael was instantly bewildered and entirely unprepared for what Mark was about to say next,

"One man's trash is another man's treasure." I wasn't quite sure whether it was an insult or a compliment.

'Oh, my hat. How trashy doesn't that sound?'

"I thought you were visiting your parents in Water Hills?"

Michael ignored him and seemed to grow increasingly agitated by Mark's cockiness.

"I was, but had to come back for … well, I just had to come back. And … in case you're wondering, my folks think you're a dick."

Michael literally huffed and puffed in front of me before he took Lily's hand and disappeared around the corner. I could only guess that they were headed into another private room, possibly a hall that was exclusively reserved for a combined bachelor's and bachelorette's. Typical of Lily. Typical of Michael.

"My ex-husband has no manners. I'm sorry he was so rude to you."

"Aah, I'm used to these motherfuckers."

'Oh my.'

Alice VL

I DO (NOT) – ABOVE THE LAW

"So, you're divorced then?"

"Yep, a few months back. The two of them were canoodling behind my back."

Mark erupted into laughter and placed his hand in front of his mouth,

"He left you for *her*?"

"Well, technically, I left him after catching them in *my* bed, but he basically has not left me alone since."

"Oh?"

'Should I tell him about Michael?'

"I'm not exactly innocent either. I took revenge on him and if you must now all the sordid details, I sort-of seduced him, and left him tied to my bed posts, blindfolded, semi-naked before I called Lily ... his girlfriend, now his bride-to-be."

Mark broke out in a kind of laughter that reminded me of ripples in a pond after a stone was thrown in which soon turned into waves of great hilarity. The sound of him laughing was contagious and instantly drew me in. I couldn't help but giggle like a little girl when he bent forward and clutched his stomach.

Alice VL

His eruption of pure glee was like an auditory hug for me. I somehow guessed that he thought it was un-manly to laugh so uncontrollably, but he just couldn't help himself and he didn't apologize for doing so.

"He obviously had a story ready for Lily, because she's still with him."

"He is such a dumb fuck." Mark was unable to control his animation. *'Oh Lawd.'*

The remainder of the evening was spent with my ankles crossed and my knees resting against the coffee table in front of us. I watched Mark often and made a determined effort to restrict myself and refrain from touching him or running my fingers through his hair. I ended up rubbing my hands often, fiercely desperate to prevent them from surrendering.

I couldn't help but inspect Mark's every movement and was often yanked back to reality by enormous sighs that would escape through my mouth. There was something about Mark that was dangerous, but it also made me feel young and free, although, not in a childlike way.

He awoke something inside of me that made me want to dance on the edge of a bridge, or tiptoe dangerously on the roof of a twenty-story building. There was a sense of adventure and jeopardy that excited me and it made my heart flicker just thinking about it.

Everything about him was *wrong*. He looked tired, worn and disheveled with scars on his hands, and one on his forehead that reminded me of a soldier sent to war. Yet, to me, Mark Warren looked stunning in a rough sort of way. He made me laugh, he promised excitement and more thrills than I was sure, I could handle.

Mark Warren knew he was attractive, but he had a way about him that made it clear; he couldn't give a damn what anyone thought of the way he looked or sounded.

He came across as the perfect rebel and it was more than likely that he would be taken seriously only once it was too late. I realized right there that Mark hated rules and would seek out boundaries simply because they needed breaking.

There was likely no rule made that he wouldn't shatter while marching to his own beat. There was a controlled chaos about him that intrigued me, and scared me a little all at the same time.

Alice VL

I DO (NOT) – ABOVE THE LAW

PART 2

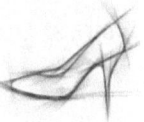

Bianca and I met up at the mall the following Tuesday evening. That evening though, we decided against a movie and instead, made our way into a coffee shop that served freshly baked scones, cupcakes and cakes.

I couldn't help but nervously glance around me often. I didn't want to run into Daniel and Lucy, but then again, I was dying to catch a glimpse of him. I just didn't want *him* to see *me*.

We found a coffee table at the outer section of the Café. I am still not sure if I had deliberately chosen that spot, or if it was simply because the coffee shop was filled with what seemed to be a bunch of pretentious women, the kind I have never felt comfortable around. Almost like swimwear models without the charm.

"So, have they managed to find out who set the fire?"

Bianca stirred her coffee before she sliced a chunk out of her serving of red velvet cake that was smothered in frosting. My slice of carrot cake appeared a little drab and tasteless next to hers.

"No. I met up with Mark at Club Zero the other night. He thought they might be there ..."

"Mark is it?"

She interrupted me with a grin indicating suspicion on her face.

"Yes. Detective Mark Warren."

"So? Were the suspects there?"

"There was a group that he spotted, but we weren't sure where and if at all, they fit in with the fire."

"*We*, is it?"

"Oh Bianca. *Stop* it."

"So, what's he like?"

"I don't know. He is a bit of a mystery."

"A mystery? How?"

"I mean, he is horribly attractive in a roughish sort of way, but a little stand-offish. He is very independent, casual, nonchalant and I can almost guarantee you, somewhere in there is a bit of a temper."

"Why do you say that?"

"Not that I've seen anything, but I get the feeling he gets what he wants."

"Oh?"

"The plan was to be undercover, and when the gang showed up, I got on his lap and pretended to lap dance for him when it seemed as though one of the gangster guys recognized him."

"Oh Ally, you surprise me more and more each day."

"Anyway, we ended up doing it right there."

Bianca almost choked on her cake and dropped her fork on her plate,

"You what?"

"I *know*. I don't really know how it happened, but we did it right there in the night club, sitting across from this whole group of gangsters. Of course, and I *hope* nobody saw, but it was over so quickly, my head spun."

"God, Ally."

"That's not all; wait till you here what happened next. Michael and Lily showed up minutes, as in seconds after we were over with ... you know? Apparently, their combined bachelor and bachelorettes was held there that night."

Bianca frowned before she picked up her fork again,

"You didn't tell me they're getting married?"

"I didn't *know*! I found out that night and at that very moment."

I took a sip of my coffee and a bite out of my carrot cake.

"There was something so confrontational about Mark, almost as though he was provoking Michael when he met him. I don't quite know how to explain it."

"What do you mean?"

"I don't know? Maybe I was just seeing things but when he found out Michael was my ex-husband, his attitude completely changed."

"Well, you can't blame him. Michael is not a likeable guy."

"Yeah, he was rather rude to Mark. But Bianca, my mama always says that if you can't see anything in someone's eyes, it's *not* a good sign."

"Well, I say you just met the guy and it was dark."

"Yep. I suppose you're right."

I didn't want to tell her that he scared and intimidated me slightly, and that I really had no idea why? His gaze was probably what unnerved me the most; that and his weapon in his holster.

But, what I couldn't deny was that I was attracted to him and I wasn't quite sure if it was his rough exterior or even rougher inner part of him that was drawing me to him like a magnet.

"Hello ladies …"

Bianca and I both looked up when we heard Daniel's voice, who by then was standing at our table. I swallowed as swiftly as I could, before I took a quick sip of my coffee.

"Hello you firefighter *you*."

'Bianca. Oh Lord.'

"Hi Daniel …"

Alice VL

Daniel smiled a sincerely sweet kind of smile with a touch of shyness lurking in his eyes. The crinkle of his dimples in the furrow of his cheeks was followed by a warm glow of joy in his eyes, almost like a ray of sunshine that was glistening over him.

He was *nothing* like Mark. Mark was *nothing* like Daniel. He was dressed in his trademark Levi jeans with a black T-shirt and a leather jacket that seemed as the exact same shade as his hair.

"Are you coming or going?"

'Why did I ask him that?'

"I'm meeting Lucy for a movie."

Lucy *woozy. Whatever.*

I was instantly disappointed and when I glanced over at Bianca, she was glaring at me.

"You ladies have fun. Nice seeing you two again."

"Have fun."

Bianca shot a toothy smile at him where I on the other hand, put an enormous effort into giving him the very best fake grin I could. I hadn't quite figured out how to turn my forged smile into a smile that could convince anybody.

Alice VL

I was terrible at it and when Daniel glowered, I knew he detected the dishonesty behind it.

"Sheez Ally."

"What?"

"That was a very, very bad imitation."

"No, it wasn't." I was desperate to defend myself and pass of my smile as authentic.

"Are you kidding me? Even someone who doesn't know you could see right through you."

"Whatever."

"When are you going to admit that you are falling for him. Or *have* fallen for him?"

"I *haven't*. There is nothing to admit. I have not fallen for Daniel Sotherby. Period."

"I have known you for a long time. You are in love with that fireman."

"I *like* him, Bianca. I'm not in love with him."

"You are going to miss your chance with him because you are too stubborn to admit it."

Alice VL

Was Bianca, right? Had I fallen in love with Daniel? I didn't know much while staring at her, but what I did know was that I just couldn't go down that road again. I didn't want to have my heart broken again.

Yet, as Daniel walked away from us, it felt as though time had collapsed into one tiny speck. My days secretly began with him and my nights secretly ended with him on my mind.

Maybe Bianca *was* right, but maybe, she was *wrong*. I didn't want to take that chance. I didn't want to devote myself to *one* man again and I wasn't ashamed to admit it. More than anything, I didn't want to give someone the power to break my heart again.

I am Ally Bradshaw. I am strong and there was no way in this lifetime that I was ever going to risk loving only one man again, just to be broken again and turned back into the same pathetic, fragile excuse of a woman I was with Michael.

'No.'

I was wiser than I was a year ago. I had lived long enough to realize that I couldn't and didn't ever want to replicate the years spent with Michael.

Alice VL

I DO (NOT) – ABOVE THE LAW

I was my own protector and I liked my life exactly the way it was. I no longer wanted to be a coward who sacrificed everything to save myself from aloneness, even at the price of emotional death. I *knew* failure; I had failed my marriage and myself. *It wasn't for me.* I wanted to stroll into a bar or a night club whenever I felt like it, and alone if I wanted to. I wanted to sing out loud to songs I love despite being off-key or tone deaf.

The four walls of my prison with Michael became a cocoon I wrapped myself in and regarded as a sanctuary rather than an incarceration. For the first time in my life, I was living a life of my own choosing.

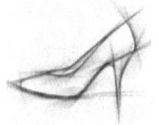

Alice VL

On Thursday morning, I woke up once again to my mobile phone's harsh and relentless ringtone. It was a little after seven, and when I reached for my phone, I was slightly unprepared to recognize the precinct's number on my screen.

"Hello?"

"Good morning, beautiful."

"Morning …"

Mark's voice was as coarse as fragmented rock grinding against each other, yet, it wholly complimented his rugged complexion.

"I've brought someone in for questioning. Can you come by and see if you recognize him?"

"Sure. Can you give me an hour?"

"Yep. No problem."

It was early, and I was still on holiday. I was looking forward to sleeping in, but at the same time, it was vital to try and identify the gang and put the arsonists behind bars.

After a quick shower, I threw on a summer dress, and grabbed a sweater from my closet. Slipping into a pair of Tomy sneakers, I hurriedly brushed my hair and braided it before applying mascara and lipstick.

When I reached the precinct, a young constable showed me into a small, dark room with nothing but a mirror separating me from what I guessed to be another interrogation room. The fluorescent light was brighter than the light in the room Daniel and I met him in only a few days before.

Mark was sitting across from a young, Latino man who didn't seem at all familiar to me. The same constable opened the door to the interrogation room and signaled for Mark to suspend the investigation.

The door to the room I was waiting in suddenly opened, and when Mark walked in, he closed it and latched the door all in one motion.

"Hello beautiful …"

He walked up to me and turbulently, kissed me. There was something unsettling about his scent and there was something chaotic about his fragrance that had me on edge straight away.

I couldn't quite figure out if his breath was that of mint mixed with strawberries, or the remnants of mint flavored chewing gum. Still, his scent was an easy fragrance, not too heavy, but magnetic at the same time.

I wrapped my arms around him and embraced his warm, welcoming lips against mine. The way his lips were pressed against mine sent immediate and unexpected shudders down my spine. It was demanding, passionate and fiery. A part of me wanted to pull away from him, but I *didn't*.

"Ally ..."

He hoarsely whispered and seduced my senses with ease. I savored his lips against mine as my heart began to flutter, and my hands began to judder.

His hands glided down to my hips before they settled around me. He pulled me closer before I inhaled abruptly.

"Thanks for coming ..."

"Sure. Is this the guy?"

My breathing had quickened as did his. I turned around and glanced over at the young man sitting in silence. Mark shifted in behind me and folded his arms around me.

"Does he look familiar to you?"

Alice VL

He didn't and the longer I looked at him, the less familiar he seemed.

"No. I don't think I've ever seen him before?"

"You sure?"

I turned around again and placed my arms around his neck. I was completely unprepared for that moment. His arms around me were stronger than any arms I had ever had around me before; it was almost as though holding me wasn't enough.

"Positive." I whispered hoarsely while the world suddenly disintegrated around me.

I leaned in and kissed him again. There were sudden and unexpected fireworks, tingles and an inexplicable desire for his roughness. His four or five-day old beard was prickly against my skin, but I didn't care. This man could kiss the life out of me.

I hesitated for a moment and looked up at him. Mark pressed himself against me before he gently shoved me into the two-way mirror. As our lips crushed together, he lifted my dress and grabbed me around my hips. My entire body clamped up as I pressed myself against him.

When he reclaimed his hand, he undid his trousers and pushed himself against me once more. With breathless anticipation, he lifted me up before my legs clamped firmly around him.

He moved slowly, but solidly. Each time he moved, his grip around me grew stronger. With each shift he made, he pushed me aggressively into the two-way mirror. I felt a rush of euphoric bliss envelop me.

I opened my mouth, prepared to belt out a loud whimper before his mouth covered mine again. It was passionate. *Intense.* It was quick and volcanic. Almost brutal.

I grabbed onto his shirt and was once again aware of a restricted kind of pleasure that was about to strike. I pulled at his shirt and gasped for air. My heart was pounding, my stomach was turning, and my breathing had become labored.

Unlike any other time before, loiteredI held my breath in anticipation of the sparks I knew were beginning to light up inside of me. The longer I held my breath, the more intense the rush inside of me was growing. I realized very quickly that the secret to an intense thrill with Mark was to hold my breath for as long as I could.

Each time I exhaled, I was aware of the buzz diminishing slightly. Hundreds of fabulous, tingling sensations disappeared by the simple act of exhaling. I was frantic to take in my next breath;

I DO (NOT) – ABOVE THE LAW

I was desperate to reclaim the uproar that threatened to stay away for good, but each time they returned, they came back stronger and more intense than before.

I was slowly beginning to get the hang of the essence of Mark and when he pressed himself against me one more time, I took in a deep breath and held forcefully onto him.

His shirt was tearing in my hands as an intense, overwhelming, untaught passionate reaction began cleaving through me as I unintentionally ripped his shirt off him.

I was panting as I desperately tried to hold my breath for just a moment longer. Mark began contracting and pulsating just as my sensations were beginning to dwindle. There was at once no sensitivity or sense to remind me that I had just hiked up a mountain peak minutes before.

It was gone. Over. *Just like that.*

Mark's prods were slower, tensed and by the way he was breathing, I knew he was about to reach his peak. His entire body convulsed and within seconds, it was over. *Gone.* As though it never was. There was no gasping, no lingering sensation, no shuddering and no throbbing that loitered.

Alice VL

I DO (NOT) – ABOVE THE LAW

There were no side effects, no flushed cheeks or drawn-out gasps of air. It was simply as though nothing at all had just happened. Don't get me wrong. *It was good.* Really good, but it was far too intense and far too abrupt. It was another new; *another* first. It turned out to be just one more thing that I was discovering for the very first time.

Maybe it was as a result of being in the precinct, surrounded by hundreds of officers of the law. Perhaps the rush and intensity was due to the realization that we *could* be caught. I had so much to discover still.

"Well, Miss Bradshaw. Thank you for coming in."

"Thank you, detective. Sorry I couldn't be of any assistance."

"Oh no, Miss Bradshaw, you were fabulous."

I giggled and picked my handbag up from the floor. This rough, tough and selfish detective turned out to be the brashest of the lot.

'I should be careful what I wish for.'

Mark walked me out of the precinct and when we reached the steps of the parking area, I couldn't miss a heart-stopping call of my name,

Alice VL

I DO (NOT) – ABOVE THE LAW

"Ally!"

Daniel. *Shit.* My heart missed far too many beats because of that damn fireman. I didn't want to turn around. I was afraid that he would once again, see right through me.

I was terrified that he would know instinctively what had just happened in a tiny, dark little room with Mark's hands all over me. I could hear Daniel's steps closing in on me, and reluctantly, I turned around, wanting to run for the hills but instead, I smiled.

"Hey Danny ..."

He was dressed in his uniform and it was spotless. There was no way in the world I could deny how fabulous he looked standing in front of me. Once again, I was completely thrown by the expression in his eyes. I suddenly realized without a shred of doubt that Daniel *could* see right through me.

He stepped back slightly, grimaced faintly before staring blankly at me. *That scent.* I had no clue of how to deal with his odor, or how I was going to remain sober around that haunting scent of his.

The fresh smell of rains in a forest lingered in the air and was like a shot of adrenaline right through my heart. The

Alice VL

butterflies in my stomach recognized him too, and begin fluttering throughout my entire being.

"Hey Daniel ..." Mark moved in next to me and smiled at Daniel.

There was a look of instant agitation on Daniel's face and when he turned to Mark, he glared suspiciously at him.

"Hi buddy ..."

"We just asked Ally to come in and see if she could identify a perp."

For some reason, I was convinced that Mark felt a sudden need to explain my presence. *'Could he see it too?'*

"Oh?"

Daniel frowned and shamelessly gawked at me.

"It wasn't anybody I've seen before ..."

Even though I was telling him the truth, well, a half-truth, the expression in his eyes was making me feel like a liar.

"Alright well ... I wanted to see you about another fire out in Kingsway ... I know it's not your jurisdiction, but I thought you could have a look and see if there are any similarities?"

Daniel turned back to Mark and handed him a stack of papers, which I assumed to be reports.

"Sure …"

I didn't know what else to say to him, and I had no inclination of what to do next. All I really wanted at that very moment was to go home, and soak in a long, hot bath.

"I better be off."

I glanced bashfully at them, not wanting to look either the fireman or the detective in the eye. I was afraid that looking at Mark would expose my involvement with him, and glancing over at Daniel might expose what I was desperately trying to hide and deny not only to the world, but to me.

"Thank you for coming in on such short notice, Miss Bradshaw. I'll be in contact."

'Nod Ally.' I nodded and waved at both Mark and Daniel.

"Bye."

From the look in Daniel's eyes, I knew I made no sense to him and by the irritation in his voice when he addressed Mark, I knew that he felt betrayed. 'He knows.'

Alice VL

I DO (NOT) – ABOVE THE LAW

I was overcome with a fear that had suddenly crept up on me when I considered what my mama always says, '*what a thin line we walk between love and hate.*' What if his affection for me ultimately turned to hatred? The very thought that Daniel might despise me felt like a knife piercing into the very core of me as I reflected on the expression in his eyes that once carried purpose and adoration, but was now filled with disgust and revolt.

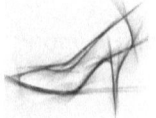

Alice VL

PART 3

On Friday morning, I literally rolled out of bed and quickly threw on a track pants and a sweater. My mobile phone had been quiet with not as much as a whisper from Daniel or from Mark.

I had just poured myself a cup of coffee when the spell of silence was instantly broken. I made myself comfortable on a stool in my kitchen at the counter, and quickly scrolled down to my messages.

'Aah. Bianca.'

"Ally wally. How about a movie tonight?"

That was exactly what I needed; a good movie and a girls night out with Bianca.

"Sounds great, but I get to pick?"

There was no way in the world I was going to allow Bianca to be choosing a movie. Besides, I was desperate to have my thoughts absorbed by the big screen. I didn't want to be

Alice VL

distracted by the fact that Daniel was six floors up. Daniel and Lucy *woozy*.

For just a second, I was beaten by emotions of what was threatening to turn into a broken relationship with Daniel while being haunted by the look in his eyes at the precinct. I shuddered and hated to admit that he was looking at me as though I was a stranger. I never sought to hurt Daniel, and I couldn't help but feel a twinge of anguish myself.

Daniel was fun and safe to be around. He catered to my every need, physically and emotionally, but somehow, I managed to destroy it all with my inability to choose him. *I didn't want to choose.* I didn't want commitment and the inevitable vulnerability that would come along with it.

But, in the same breath, I didn't want Lucy to have him either. I didn't want her to be the woman he gave his heart to. To me, she was a viper, and quite possibly, the best-looking girl in town. *'Urgh'*

"Fine. See you at eight?"

"See you there."

I had just begun sipping on my coffee when there was a sudden and unexpected knock on my front door. There was no one in the world that should have been at my door at that very moment, or at that time of the morning.

Having learnt my lessons in the past, I peered through the keyhole and was not at all surprised to find Michael standing there.

'What a damn cheek.'

I tried to peer past him to see if Lily had accompanied him, but I couldn't see her anywhere. He was alone, and I couldn't for the life of me imagine what he wanted from me at that very moment, and especially, after all that had happened between us. I did my best to hide my irritation and opened the door,

"Michael? Seriously, this has to stop."

Without saying a word, he brushed past me and scurried over into my living room. I was stunned but at the same time, I couldn't ignore the unanticipated desolation on his face.

I was certainly not in the mood for his whining, but I closed the door behind him, and walked on over to where he was standing. When I took a seat across from him, he sat down slowly before I carried on sipping my coffee.

"I owe you an apology, Ally."

Alice VL

Wait. Hang on. I almost spat out my coffee and was not entirely sure I had heard Michael correctly. *'Where is this coming from?'* I was stunned, speechless and lost for words. I was not sure what brought on his sudden change of heart and while flabbergasted by his apology, I chose to remain silent.

'This is going to be good.'

"I mean, I didn't think you'd ever really leave me. I treated you unfairly for most of our marriage, and then that *thing* with Lily … I just don't know what got into me? I honestly never, ever thought you'd divorce me."

"It wasn't a *thing* with Lily, Michael. It was an affair. You're making no sense … what are you trying to say, *exactly*?"

"I'm saying I made a mistake."

Without running the risk of spilling my coffee all over me, I placed my mug on the coffee table.

"I don't know what you want me to say?"

Michael gazed incredulously at me, as though he was expecting me to run back into his cheating arms. At the same time, I could see traces of a man defeated, discomposed and tattered.

Alice VL

I DO (NOT) – ABOVE THE LAW

I felt sorry for him, but I simply no longer loved him, not that I ever really did. I didn't want him back and I certainly did not want to hear how anguished he was.

"I want you to know that I'm sorry. For Lily, for your parents, for *everything*. I was a terrible husband."

'That you sure were.'

Instead of responding to his desperate apology, I bowed my head in a frantic attempt to refrain from lashing out at him. I so badly wanted to agree with him and blurt out how pathetic he was. With each word Michael was proclaiming his remorse with, I grew progressively angrier. I wanted to do nothing more than bark at him while allowing the rage I felt towards him to destroy him and consume all that he was and ever would be. I wanted to humiliate him and disclose that I never loved him, but *I didn't.*

"It is what it is Michael, and we both need to move forward."

Michael lowered his head and began fidgeting nervously before he gazed up at me,

"Is there any way, Ally? Is there any chance for us to try again?"

'Oh Lord. No. No. No.'

Alice VL

I didn't want to come across as cruel, especially after the fiasco we only recently found ourselves in, but I definitely did not want to go down that road again.

"I don't understand, Michael? You and Lily are getting married ... you just celebrated your bachelor's party?"

"Yeah ... about that ..."

I honestly didn't want to hear what he had to say about it, and before he could spin me some or other sob story, I cut him off at once.

"Listen Michael ... it hurt when you cheated on me. It really came crashing down on me like a ton of bricks would, especially since you were my first at everything, and especially because I devoted myself to a lifetime with you. But in all honesty, I was never really *happy*, and I don't think you were either? I am at such a good place right now, and it has made me realize that you and I didn't love each other. We simply loved the *idea* of each other. I don't want to try again, I like my life exactly as it is right now."

"I can change, Ally?"

"No Michael, that wouldn't be fair. You are who you are and for another woman, like Lily for example, you are perfect, but not for me. And, I'm not saying this to hurt you, I don't … I just don't love you and I don't want to be tied down again."

Michael shook his head and looked away, before he got up and made his way to my front door. He was sadder leaving my apartment than he was when he first walked in. I felt terrible. *Guilty*.

I didn't want to be responsible for another person's pain, but I didn't want Michael Bradshaw back in my life, or back in my bed. All I had to do was picture his purplish, old and scrawny true him, and my decision was instantly justified.

"I want you to be happy Michael. Give Lily a fair chance, she's a lot like you."

Michael turned around when he opened my front door. I knew him well and I knew he was embarrassed. *Humiliated*. Michael was about to leave *without* what he came for and it was a first for him. From the dejected expression on his face, I was sure that rejecting him, almost killed him.

"This is your last chance, Ally. I am not going to wait for you or ask you again." I wanted to burst out laughing, instead I swallowed back as best as I could. Still, I couldn't wipe a devious grin from my face.

Alice VL

"I understand, Michael. That will be on me and I'll probably live to regret it for the rest of my life."

Michael was about to step through my front door, when Mark suddenly appeared out of nowhere. He frowned when he spotted Michael on his way out. Michael pouted and grimaced when he realized the rough detective was on his way in. I bowed my head, unsure of how to justify one another to either of them.

For some unexplained and totally unexpected reason, I felt as though I was cheating on both.

"Mark?"

"Hi. I uhm … got your address from the case docket at the precinct."

Michael turned ashen and looked Mark squarely in the eye,

"Aren't you the dude from Club Zero the other night?"

Mark leaned against the wall and smiled. It wasn't a normal, regular or friendly smile. It was rather clear that there was nothing amicable about him at that very moment. I was beginning to feel intimidated and increasingly unnerved.

"Yes, the very same dude."

Alice VL

Michael turned back to me,

"Remember what I said Ally … my offer won't stand for much longer."

"Thanks Michael … like I said, I understand."

Michael walked off without saying another word. Mark turned around and watched him until he disappeared around the corner. When he turned back to me, he smiled,

"Hi."

'Oh my. How sexy is that?'

Still leaning against the wall, I couldn't help but pore over him from top to bottom. Mark was standing before me in all his grandeur. He was wearing a striped shirt with an old, faded pair of jeans. His chiseled jaw was slightly lifted with a proud and pleasant smile all of a sudden. For the first time since I met Mark, there was a sparkle in his eyes below a rich, dark brow. Yet, everything about him still felt *wrong*.

"Can I come in?"

"Sure …"

I stepped back and made way for him to enter my apartment. It suddenly struck me that this was the first man I had opened my home to. *Except Michael.* But Michael didn't count simply for the fact that I was not sleeping with him, nor will I ever again.

"I can offer you a cup of coffee?"

I closed the door behind him and quickly led him into the kitchen.

"Black, no sugar."

Suddenly my grandmother's voice was loud and I could clearly hear her say, '*throw caution to the wind when you meet the man that takes his coffee black and without sugar.*'

I poured him a cup and handed his coffee to him.

"So, to what do I owe this pleasure?"

"I was at the museum and your assistant said you were still on holiday?"

"Yep, another whole week filled with nothing."

"Anyway, the reason why I stopped in was to let you know that we're still working the case and have some leads that we are following up on."

"Why, thank you detective … I so appreciate house calls."

Alice VL

I moved closer and slid my hand in underneath his shirt. His chest wasn't as carved or sculpted as Daniel or Ryan's was, but still as hard as a rock.

"Hmm … Miss Bradshaw …"

When he stood up, I pushed him back onto the bar stool.

"This is my precinct, detective, and here my law is the only law that counts right now. I make the rules over here … and I punish law-breakers without mercy."

Mark smiled and leaned back,

"Alright captain. What do you want from me? Interrogate me all you want."

When I spotted his pistol, I was instantly alarmed, but I didn't want Mark to pick up on my sudden fear.

"Remove that thing … it's not the weapon I'm aiming for."

He looked down, and quickly unbelted his weapon before he placed it on the kitchen counter.

"That's better. Hand over your cuffs."

He obediently unclipped his cuffs and placed them on the kitchen counter.

Alice VL

I DO (NOT) – ABOVE THE LAW

"You do have keys for these, right?" I whispered with just a tad bit uncertainty.

'Just checking.'

Mark burst out laughing and nodded.

"Get up, Detective!"

He got up slowly, still smirking broadly.

"Turn around and walk slowly down the passage. Hands where I can see them …"

'Ooh, I like the way I sound.'

I grabbed the cuffs and led him into my bedroom.

"On the bed; now!"

'I sound so bad ass.'

Mark obeyed and slowly lowered himself onto my bed. As though I had been seducing and commanding men my entire life, I climbed on top of him and lifted his arms above his head before I cuffed his hands together.

"I am going to search you now. Don't move, understand?"

"Yes ma'am."

I DO (NOT) – ABOVE THE LAW

Without unbuttoning his shirt, I moved straight down to his zipper. Before pulling it down, I was distracted by an ever-growing bulge from his crotch. I gently placed my hands over his curve and squeezed tightly.

"What's hiding in here, detective? Anything to declare?"

"No ma'am."

"Detective, if I find out that you are lying to me, I will punish you severely."

"Yes, please do …"

He lifted his buttocks slightly and quivered. I pulled his zipper down and was instantly surprised to find him unexpectedly exposed. No boxers. No Jockey's. *Nothing.*

"Oh Detective. You've got some explaining to do. I warned you about lying, and now I am going to have to punish you."

"Please be kind."

Again, *'my thing'* took over as I stared at the beautiful, though slightly curved specter staring back at me. I had never seen such a flawless curve before and for a moment, I couldn't help but wonder if that was the reason for the explosive intensities that would vanish just as quickly as they appeared?

Alice VL

I DO (NOT) – ABOVE THE LAW

I grabbed at him and looked him squarely in the eye,

"Do you have a permit to carry this concealed weapon?"

'Oh Lawd. Did I just say that?'

"Fuck Ally."

'Oh my.' "You have a dirty mouth too? Watch yourself detective, you might just find yourself in prison before the day is over."

I knew Mark was highly seduced and greatly aroused. He was desperate for me to punish him rigidly and without mercy. I relented and began handing out his punishment.

"Yes, yes."

'Oh, he's a talker.'

I pinned his hands down and stirred vigorously until he began to convulse slightly. When he began moving rigorously underneath me, I pressed down on him and lifted myself off him.

"What the fuck?"

"I told you I was going to punish you dearly." He brought his hands over his head, and still cuffed, he turned me around onto my stomach, and rested himself on top of me.

Alice VL

I DO (NOT) – ABOVE THE LAW

'Well, that didn't take long?'

He relaxed his entire weight onto me and with force, he placed his cuffed hands out in front of me. There it was. That same restricted sensation that failed to send those intoxicating ripples and currents through my body and down my spine. It was all *confined*, focused and limited to an enclosed area.

The sensations were mild, slow-peaking but hit suddenly and again, without warning. I grabbed my sheets and tugged at them before I gave one and only whimper. A new kind of intensity I hadn't known, yet somehow, slightly unfulfilling and swift. *Too quick.*

It was there for a split second, and then it was *gone*. I wasn't quite sure that Detective Mark Warren was as sensual as I hoped he would be. Rough, tough and so very appealing, but not quite as *sensual*. Perhaps, it was too rushed. Maybe, too passionate. How would I know?

He got up off me and turned me around to face him.

"You get me off far too quickly."

'Hallelujah. It's nothing more than the fact that I am too sensual for him. That's my story and that is what I am sticking to.'

"Grab the keys in my left pocket."

Alice VL

I giggled and grabbed the keys to his cuffs before I quickly un-cuffed him. With his hands finally freed, he bent down and kissed me. That was the one thing this rough detective got right each time; he kissed me like he had stolen me.

"I gotta get back to the precinct. See you tonight?"

"I can't. I'm going to the movies with my friend, Bianca."

"Afterwards maybe?"

"Maybe ..."

He quickly pulled up his zipper before he bent down and kissed me again. Another one of those fabulous, sensual and addictive kisses. Hot, fiery, passionate and demanding.

The kind of kiss I couldn't pull myself away from. Mark Warren's kisses turned out to be both my salvation and my torment. If only the rest of him had the same effect.

"Oh, by the way, what did your ex want?"

"You will never believe ..."

Mark sat down on the bed beside me and when I sat upright, I took a pillow to cover myself up.

"He is sorry he cheated on me, and wants us to try to save our marriage, which I might add, is no more. He forgets we are divorced."

"Wasn't that his bachelor's the other night?"

"Yep."

"What did you say?"

"I said no. I mean, not in a bad way, but still, no."

"What a douche."

He rose to his feet and placed his arms around me. I liked how he felt. I felt invincible and special, but I didn't feel the way I felt in Daniel's arms.

'Daniel. Shit.'

"I'll call you later."

"Okay."

He kissed me on my forehead before he walked out of my bedroom. When I heard the front door close behind him, I ran down the passage and quickly locked the front door before I ran a bath. When I pulled up at the mall later that evening, I was surprised to find it eerily deserted for a Friday night. I was feeling slightly anxious and hoped with all my heart that I didn't run into

Daniel, especially not with Lucy hanging onto him. *'I honestly don't like that girl.'*

When I hesitantly walked through the glass doors of the mall, I was pleased to discover that larger than normal crowds were lining up in front of the movie theatre. I was relieved and knew that crowds like that would allow me to disappear into the hordes and make myself far too small for Daniel to notice me.

"Ally ..."

'Oh no. Seriously?'

I turned around and looked smack-bang into Daniel's face.

'No Lucy?'

"Hi."

He must have been coming off shift as he too, was making his way into the mall still dressed in his fireman's uniform. Only this time, he reeked of smoke and looked as though he had been through the ringer.

"Did you just come off shift?"

"Yep, it was a long day."

"Are you alright?"

My heart just about sank to my feet when I saw smudges of soot on his face and in his hair.

"Two fires today. Similar to the one at the museum, only the last one had two fatalities."

Daniel's eyes were glistening. He was upset and it looked as though he had aged ten years. I took a step forward desperate to get a closer look at him. He looked both young and old at the same time.

I couldn't deny the apparent pain and hidden trauma in his eyes. He suddenly looked old, but still, I could see the young fireman I had fallen in lust with. There were worry-lines across his forehead I had never seen before and it scared me. It was in moments like those that Daniel would come to me, almost ghost-like. Moments where he was desperate to walk tall, but was beaten down.

A fine layer of grey ash had settled onto his uniform and boots. It upset me tremendously to see Daniel as fragile as he was at that very moment. His shoulders were slumped while his eyes were sad and discouraged. My eyes suddenly became glazed as a glassy layer of tears threatened to roll onto my cheeks the moment I blinked.

"I'm so sorry, Danny. Are you okay?"

Alice VL

"Yep, I guess."

I wanted to wrap him in my arms and hold him tightly against me. I wanted to kiss him gently and promise him that the world was not such a bad place. I wanted Daniel Sotherby to know that I *cared*.

I wanted to tell him that I couldn't stand seeing the sadness in his eyes, or the broken and worn look on his face. I wanted to tell him that it hurt and that my heart loved him.

'No. It doesn't.'

Instead, I placed a hand on his cheek, and gently wiped a smudge of root from his face. His eyes gazed into mine and for a split-second, I saw my life and future in Daniel's eyes. I could see right through them and the pain that I found there, debilitated me and shattered pieces of my soul. I was overcome with a nagging sensitivity that his eyes were windows trying to show me my way home.

"There you are!"

Lucy bloody *woozy*.

"Are you okay, baby?"

'Baby?'

Alice VL

I DO (NOT) – ABOVE THE LAW

She placed her arms around his neck and held him for what felt like forever. Somehow, I knew that Lucy would become the girl I would love to hate for years to come. Daniel wrapped his arms around her and rested his head on her shoulders before he closed his eyes.

'Baby?'

"I have to go ... I am meeting Bianca ..."

I walked backwards. I felt awkwardly out of place, like an unwelcomed stranger. I didn't belong there. I had no right to stand there and watch him disappear into her arms. I didn't want to.

"Bye."

I turned around and did my best to disappear into the crowd. I didn't hear Daniel acknowledge my departure, and I did not wait to see him wave me goodbye. I wanted to be gone from him; the him that included Lucy. I wanted to be angry with him to protect me from the pain I was feeling. I was desperate to summon the strength to walk away, and stay away from Daniel, but I was failing myself and I was deserting my heart.

When I spotted Bianca, I engaged in a valiant effort to wipe the sorrow from my heart and from my face. My heart was thrashing ferociously, and my hands were shuddering heartlessly.

"Hey … what's the matter? It looks like you've seen a ghost?"

"Nothing … I'm just a little flustered. The crowds …"

"Yeah, well … I got our tickets. I've got us seats for that new engine-petrol dude."

Wait. What? I stared at Bianca, unable to place this engine-petrol dude she so proudly got us tickets for.

"Engine Petrol … those car action movies."

That was all I needed to snap out of the gloom I had suddenly found myself in. I laughed so hard, my legs were beginning cave in under me. I bent down and clutched my belly as the tears began streaming down my face.

'Bianca. Ai jai jai.'

"What's so funny? I thought you'd like that movie?"

"I do, I really, really do like those movies. I thoroughly enjoy the action scenes, but the engine-petrol dude is actually called Vin Diesel."

"Whatever. I knew it was something car'*ish.*"

Alice VL

I DO (NOT) – ABOVE THE LAW

I placed my hand on her shoulder and lifted myself up, still laughing so loudly, the entire crowd began staring at us. I couldn't help it; there are just some things in life you cannot keep veiled and this was one of them.

We found our seats in the third row in the already darkened and quiet movie theatre. Bianca and I both ordered an extra-large popcorn and soda. When we were comfortable, and the opening credits began, I sat back and couldn't help but see Daniel's eyes in front of me. How was it possible that his eyes were so permanently burnt into my mind?

There was a sadness in them I had never seen before. A kind of desperation that scared and altogether unnerved me. It was a look I had never seen before, and I knew that I never wanted to see it again. It reminded me of a vulnerability and a kind of failure that nobody deserved to feel.

I wanted to hold him, *love* him and protect him. I wanted to stand beside him and pick up the pieces *with* him. I wanted to sit close to him and hold his hand. I wanted to tell Daniel Sotherby that the world was a much better place *because* of him. I wondered when last someone might have told him that he mattered? Not just mattered, but that he was extraordinary. I want to do that. *Me.*

Alice VL

I wanted, more than anything in the world, to tell Daniel that he was so very larger than life in my extremely small world.

"See you later ..." It was a whisper behind me that caught me off-guard at once. I turned around and immediately caught a glimpse of Mark in the row behind me. I was instantly unnerved and couldn't help but feel somewhat defenseless and exposed.

'Is he following me?'

Never before had I felt as intimidated and imposed on as I had at that very moment. There was a demoralizing outrage, entitlement and jurisdiction in his voice that immensely frightened and exhausted me.

I wanted to leave. My first instinct was to escape the movie theatre. My heart was clattering as though it would pound right out of my chest.

"Don't turn around ..."

I turned back instantly and stared blankly at the big screen in front of me. For the first time since meeting Mark, I was afraid. I couldn't quite put my finger on it, but there was something suddenly not quite right with Detective Mark Warren.

He didn't say a word after that and when I turned around slowly, he was gone. For a moment, I thought I might have imagined him behind me, but the upright hairs on my neck made it terrifyingly real to me.

I turned to Bianca who was wholly engrossed in the movie in front of her, entirely oblivious to the short and unexpected visit from Mark.

Again, I could feel the blood drain from my face and I could in no way at all, shake the feeling of being watched. I had never been stalked before and I was not quite sure if I was being paltry by labeling it.

When the movie was over, needless to say, I had barely watched ten minutes involving a gorgeous FBI agent and an equally smoldering thug in a fast-paced, action-packed thriller. Bianca swooned and couldn't get enough of the roaring engines, full-throttle races and heart-stopping heartthrobs.

"If I knew these dudes were so hot, I would happily have watched these movies with you, Ally."

With Mark still on my mind, I smiled and while completely crushed by fear, I had no desire to go home.

"Do you feel like a late dinner?" I didn't want to go home just yet.

Alice VL

"I mean, I would … and I'd love to normally but, I actually have a date tonight …"

Bianca. *Dating*? I was not prepared for that.

"You do?"

She giggled shyly,

"I do. I'll call you tomorrow; we're going out to some or other Club Zero …"

"Oh, I know that place. It's where Mark and I was … it's great."

"His name is Fabio, an Italian dude I met when I designed his company website for him."

I placed my arms around her and hugged her tightly.

"Be careful, okay?"

"Okay."

Bianca turned and dashed through the glass doors of Willow County Mall. I stood as though frozen in time, not sure of where to go or what to do with myself. Perhaps, I was just over-reacting. After all, Mark Warren was an officer of the law.

Alice VL

I DO (NOT) – ABOVE THE LAW

Perhaps, he just *genuine*ly liked me. Once I had successfully convinced myself that I was being nothing more than paranoid and petty, I climbed into my car and drove back to my apartment.

When I pulled up at the apartment building, the parking lot was eerily quiet and dark. I had never really noticed how haunting it was that late at night. Something in the air all around me did felt wide off the mark. I felt the sweat drench my skin and the thumping of my heart against my chest. My fingers were curled into a fist while my nails began digging into my palms.

I breathed quietly as I nervously glanced around me. Not only were my eyes pulsating around me, but the silence was worse than ringing screams in my ears. I had never been afraid of the dark or the eerie silence, but at that very moment, I was overcome with fear and dread.

There was no-one in sight, and when I finally climbed out of my car, the silence suddenly surrendered to the haunting sounds of footsteps that I was convinced, were approaching me. I was terrified. I could not turn around and face whatever it was that was lurking closer.

Alice VL

I DO (NOT) – ABOVE THE LAW

I suddenly felt someone slam me into my car and breathe rapidly down my neck. I couldn't hear anything else but the short breaths and the galloping of my own heart in my ears.

I did my best not to make a sound as each second went on forever. What began as a contortion of my stomach turned into a feeling of being smothered by an invisible hand.

My breathing was becoming more erratic as I desperately tried to fight the panic that had suddenly entirely engulfed me. My body warned me that it was about to shut down completely when a violent shudder consumed and weakened me. My legs were paralyzed by fear and my hands were ice cold.

"Hello beautiful …"

'Are you shitting me?'

Hearing Mark's voice did nothing to set my mind at ease. I could still barely move, and my legs were still unwilling to take flight. My hand automatically covered my chest where I could still feel the frigid cold surround my heart.

"Shit, you scared the crap out of me …"

He turned me around and slid his arms in around my waste.

"Sorry."

Alice VL

I DO (NOT) – ABOVE THE LAW

Mark pulled me closer to him and kissed me fervently. I closed my eyes, afraid of going completely numb but when his tongue frantically explored my mouth, I was once again swept up and savored the warmth of his lips against mine.

I was suddenly so drawn to the way Mark took charge and took care of business even if it was in a deserted parking lot. The fact that he scared the living daylights out of me, just made me want him even more. All my hesitation and fears of a moment ago were gone as he swept me into his arms and kissed me like I was his very first kiss.

Mark was mayhem and as much as I was being pulled in the opposite direction, I had no power to resist or abandon him. In the quietest of moments, Mark would find me almost as though he was a shadow of me. He was chaos and noise that left my emotions swirling faster than a spinning top. He stepped back and slowly unbuttoned my jeans.

"Here?"

"Why not"

Mark's passions arrived unannounced and ended explosively, like car bombs going off one by one. I glanced around me, nervous and anxious that someone might see us.

Alice VL

I DO (NOT) – ABOVE THE LAW

"It's late …"

He grabbed his pistol from his holster and jumped into the air with his arm stretched out over his head, knocking the light out above us. Suddenly, it was dark with only a faint light coming from around the corner.

He pulled my jeans down with force and instantly, pulled his down to his ankles. He picked me up and pressed me against my car before he kissed me again.

I couldn't figure out what it was about Mark that made me feel as though he was above the law. The passion was intense and my arousal instantaneous. A hunger for his roughness was something I could not ignore. There was something so beguiling and sexy about that rough detective and his way of taking control of me.

Underneath his tongue, I lost all logic and good sense. For a few moments, I was under his control and caught up in a magnetic field with him. I didn't care much about anything else other than shutting down from the world around me and being captured and entirely seized by Mark.

He pushed himself against me as he thrust against me with force. I lifted my head and arched my back when an immediate sensation began to vibrate inside of me. Maybe it was the danger of being caught, or perhaps, it was the curve of him, but at once, my entire body contracted intensely, sending strong ripples into my belly and up my spine until every part of my body broke out into a passionate shudder.

It was nothing like before. In that moment, it was highly pleasing and immensely satisfying. The orgasmic intensity I craved with Mark had finally shown up.

'That's more like it.'

Mark's grip around me was stronger as he dug his fingers into my thighs. He squeezed harder and harder. I was at once aware of his painful grip on me, but I held my breath and bit on my bottom lip, hoping it would be over soon.

With each drive, his grip increased in waves, with small lulls giving false hope of an end. Each peak robbed me of my ability to speak and all I could do was writhe with the occasional whimper echoing off the walls.

But again, just as soon as it started, it was over. Mark rested his head into my chest, and finally released his painful hold on me. He was panting and grunting and stood with his head buried in my chest for just a moment longer before he stepped back and placed me back on the ground.

Alice VL

I DO (NOT) – ABOVE THE LAW

I quickly pulled up my jeans and grabbed my handbag. Once his trousers were pulled back up, he leaned forward and kissed me.

I couldn't help but feel slightly under-valued. I was still classy and elegant, and parking lots were not my *thing*. Yet, it was thrilling and exciting, but the fact that I had to force a counterfeit smile made way for an awkward transience.

"I have to go. Apparently, there is an eye witness back at the precinct who can identify the arsonist. I'll call you, okay?"

He was finished with me after he performed like a true champion. Again, I felt tawdry. *Used*. Was this how Daniel felt? It was not something I ever wanted to feel again and at once, I understood why Daniel felt the need to punish me not too long ago. I was deceiving myself. I was acting on impulse and then created reasons to justify my actions. I was doing nothing more than hiding behind Michael and my miserable marriage to him.

I stopped thinking before I spoke or how I acted. I was thinking only about myself, my own needs and no-one else. Not once did I truly ask Daniel, or Michael for that matter, how I made *them* feel. Not once did I ask Ryan or William Walker if I made them feel lesser.

"Okay."

Alice VL

I DO (NOT) – ABOVE THE LAW

Mark turned around and quickly made his way back to his car that was parked four cars away from mine. I straightened my clothes and hurriedly made my way into the apartment building and back to my place.

I felt dirty. I felt used. I felt ugly, but, at least, I didn't feel drab or boring. Still, it was not a feeling I liked, and I realized at once that Detective Mark Warren was a little too rough for Ally Bradshaw. I was still a lady, and I wanted to be treated as such.

Without switching on any lights, I hurriedly disappeared into my bathroom and drew myself a warm bath. His smell on me was suddenly nauseating when it hit me out of the blue. He smelt like nothing more than whiskey and tobacco.

I lay in the bath thinking of Daniel and the look in his eyes only hours before. But as I lay there soaking, I knew that at that very moment, Lucy was with him and I had no doubt that *she* would happily cater to his every need.

'Bitch. Yes, Ally, you.'

I glanced over at my mobile phone and frowned when I noticed the flickering light. "You looked pretty tonight."

How was it possible that Daniel, after having such a shitty day, could still take the time to send me a message? How was his timing always so impeccable and perfect? I was flabbergasted, but happy. My heart pounded and my stomach turned. Again, I felt nauseated by my actions.

It was as though I never left his mind; I was always just there. I didn't understand him, and I couldn't make sense of who *I* was anymore. Overcome with sudden horror, it hit me; Daniel was my one stable force, the one stability I had in a world filled with chaos and clutter. The discovery stretched out through my entire body and overwhelmed me. *It scared me.* It wasn't a case that I had fallen in love with Daniel, it was a fact that I fell in love with him each time I saw him. And each time, I grew increasingly obsessed with and bewitched by him.

This was not the plan. *'This. Can. Not. Be. The. Plan.'*

"Thank you, Danny. Are you okay?"

Within seconds, his reply came back, "Yep. I snap out of things quite quickly. Shit happens. It's life and it's my job."

"Still, I am sorry. I hate that things like that happen."

Moments after I responded, Daniel replied again,

"Me too."

Without replying again, I placed my mobile phone on the edge of the tub and submerged myself fully under water. I just wanted to shut out the world around me. I wanted to think of nothing and feel *nothing*. I was spiraling into an abyss I had no control over.

With my eyes closed, I thought of my parents and of Max. I thought of Ryan and still felt guilty that I never got to say goodbye to him. More than that, I hoped he recovered swiftly from the humiliation of my last night there. I thought of William Walker and the children lucky enough to have him offer them new lives. I thought of Daniel. *Sigh*

After only a few moments more, my mind drifted to Detective Mark Warren. I knew for a fact that he terrified me. He unnerved me. When I was around him, I was blissfully consumed by him, but when I was alone, being with him made my skin crawl. My actions repulsed me. My insides curdled like milk does with lemon. I was revolted by how he made me feel. Around him, I was nothing more than a queen of a dollar note, and it wouldn't matter if I was wearing a stained dress or shoes that were chafed and worn.

Alice VL

I DO (NOT) – ABOVE THE LAW

PART 4

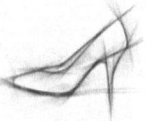

From a distance, I could hear my phone ring. I was not ready to wake up yet; I didn't quite want to face the world just yet. I was exhausted and all I wanted to do was turn around and fall asleep again.

The exhaustive ringing on my mobile phone continued to echo relentlessly in my ears as I groggily opened my eyes. It was dark all around me with nothing else but the incessant sounds coming from that awful device.

'Why didn't I put my phone on silent?'

I peered over and did in no way at all, recognize the number on the screen. It was just after 3am when I grabbed my phone and still not quite awake, I reluctantly took the call.

"Ally." I was irritated and confused.

I could hear nothing else but loud voices in the background. I was about to end the call when I heard Michael's panicky and terrified voice,

Alice VL

"It's me, Michael."

"What the fuck, Michael? It's 3am!"

"I know. I didn't know who else to call?"

There was a tremble in Michael's voice I had never heard before. I could at once detect stammering traces of fear that had me instantly wide awake.

The distress in his voice made my breathing rapid and shallow. *Something was wrong.* I could feel my pulse pounding against my temples as my hands began to shake.

Except for the voices in the background, Michael was silent. I instinctively began constructing scenarios; did something happen to my parents? Was something wrong back home? I couldn't stand his silence and felt panic well up inside me at once.

"Michael!"

I sat upright in bed, suddenly aware of a violent thud in my heart.

"Lily and I have been arrested."

Wait. What?

"What?"

I DO (NOT) – ABOVE THE LAW

"We're being held at the precinct."

"What for?"

"Arson. And drugs."

By then, I was fully awake and entirely disorientated. Michael an arsonist and a drug user?

I suddenly felt as though I had been dropped far out into the ocean and submerged below the water. I could hardly breathe and couldn't help but wonder if Michael was simply losing his mind.

"Is this a joke?"

"No Ally, it's not. Apparently, an eye witness has come forward and identified me as the one who set fire to the museum. They came in a few hours ago with a warrant and found drugs at my place …"

I was shocked. Stunned. Speechless. Michael, an arsonist *and* a junkie? In all the years I had known Michael, he despised drugs. He wouldn't even take a pain killer. I was left shocked and in disbelief. My mind was reeling, unable to process exactly what Michael was telling me.

"I swear Ally, those drugs aren't mine. Or Lily's. You know me. You *know* me, Ally."

Alice VL

"Then where did they come from?"

"I don't know … but it's that detective. I will bet my life on it he planted them there."

"What detective? Detective Warren?"

Michael remained silent. I was stunned. *'Why would Mark do that?'* It had to be a mistake. There was a sudden silence to my soul. I could feel the chill in my blood as the coldness brought my mind to a standstill.

"Why would he do that?"

"I don't know, Ally. We are only able to appear in court on Monday morning. I need a lawyer … *we* need a lawyer."

"Wait. You used your only phone call to call me?"

"I didn't know who else to call?"

Involuntarily, I shook my head violently. *'A lawyer, why didn't he call a lawyer? Why call me? What am I supposed to do?'* Michael confused and angered me, but more than anything else, there was Mark and the hand he had in putting Michael and Lily in jail.

The fear in my chest was waiting to take over like an angry ball propelling me towards anxiety. I was beginning to understand Mark and saw a perfect mask of pretense that was busy crumbling right before my eyes. I didn't know *how* to feel? There was nothing but void and numbness into the very core of me.

"A lawyer, Michael! You call a lawyer, not your ex-wife! Where's Lily now?"

"In a holding cell."

I gasped for air. I didn't like Lily, but I had known her for many years. She was as straight an arrow as Michael was. I never expected to feel so much empathy for both Michael and Lily, but I *did*. My heart felt as though a hundred knives had just pierced it.

I could hear the horror in Michael's voice and I knew without a fraction of doubt that he was innocent. Lily, on the other hand, I was not too sure about.

"You're sure they're not Lily's?"

"God Ally, you know me. You know I wouldn't put up with this shit."

"Yes, I know, I just had to ask. I don't know what I can do but let me see who I can get a hold of. When is your bail hearing?"

"On Monday morning."

Alice VL

"Are you being kept in holding until then?"

"Yeah. It looks that way."

"Okay. I'll call around for a lawyer."

"Thank you, Ally."

I ended the call, still stunned that Michael and Lily were arrested and behind bars for arson and drug charges. I was suddenly overcome by an awful feeling about Mark, almost like a nudge of caution, and I didn't quite know what to make of the unfortunate situation.

I climbed out of bed and got dressed as swiftly as I could. Without a drop of make-up on, I brushed my hair, grabbed my coat, my mobile phone and keys. As though in a wandering haze, I drove out to the precinct, hoping that Mark was on duty. When I walked in, I spotted him straight away.

"I was going to call you in the morning ... we made an arrest in the arson case."

"I know ... can we talk?"

Mark placed a protective, yet unsettling arm around me and led me back into the interrogation room. He pulled out a chair for me before he walked over and sat down across from me.

I DO (NOT) – ABOVE THE LAW

"An eye witness identified your ex-husband, Michael as the arsonist. We searched his place and in the process, we found large amounts of narcotics; cocaine, Ecstasy pills, needles and an ice pipe."

I was stunned. There was no way in the world that Michael would ever do drugs, or sell drugs. It was no secret that he was pathetic and irritating, but he was not an arsonist or a junkie and neither was Lily. Something about Mark's account of what had happened felt completely wrong. I suddenly felt as though I was trapped in a war zone between the truth and twisted lies, and Mark Warren was hiding the truth so skillfully.

"Listen Mark … I don't know who that eye witness is, but Michael isn't capable of setting fire to anything. He's never even gotten a parking ticket in his entire life."

Mark reached for my hand and clutched it into his. His eyes were narrowed, rigid, cold and lifeless. I suddenly felt like the enemy and it baffled me even more. I took in a deep breath. I didn't want him to detect the fear that suddenly conquered me as his burning stare lasted for far too long.

I got the feeling that I somehow crossed an invisible line with him and offended him in the process. I had never been afraid of a man before, but I was suddenly feeling vulnerable and downright isolated.

"I don't know what to say, Ally? He was picked in a line-up. The witness was quite clear about what he saw and identified Michael Bradshaw as the perpetrator and without any hesitation."

"It *has* to be a mistake, Mark. And the drugs? Michael is a straight arrow. He has never used drugs in all the years that I've known him. *Never.*"

"All I can say Ally, is that we found the drugs in his apartment. Maybe it was his girlfriend's … I don't know? But, in the end, his name is on the lease and the drugs as well as the needles and pipe was found in his home."

"No Mark, *not* even Lily. Lily wouldn't do drugs and Michael wouldn't allow it in his apartment. I *know* him, Mark."

Again, there was a deadness, a certain stillness to his eyes. There was a look I could only imagine was reserved for prisoners. It was a hateful kind of disdain. There was a tenseness he wasn't even trying to mask and nothing much made sense to me at that very moment. There was no getting through to Mark and as his hands curled into fists, the anger radiated from his skin. There was nothing more I could think of saying to try and convince him of their innocence, and when I noticed a blank look in his eyes, I knew instinctively that I was on my own.

"All I can suggest Ally, is that he hires himself a good attorney. It's not looking so good for either of them. But at least now, *now* he can't bother you anymore …"

Wait. Hang on. Did he just say that? Did Mark set him up? *'Why?'*

There was a look in Mark's eyes that scared me almost to death. One of satisfaction; one of pleasure. I was sure that I detected a hint of gratification beneath the surface of his hardened expression. Was it possible that Mark had framed Michael?

I stood up and quickly made my way to the door. I didn't want Mark to sense my discomfort, but at the same time, I couldn't spend a moment more in his company.

His gaze was like a knife in my ribs, digging deeper and deeper. Where there once was lust and passion, was now an emptiness filled with outrage and raw anger. Revulsion was beginning to overpower me when I considered a painful reality that Mark *wanted* Michael out the way.

"I'll walk you out …"

Alice VL

I turned back, fraught to flash Mark a convincing smile. I had no idea what he was capable of and I was beginning to see a side to him that beleaguered me. There was a kind of danger about Detective Mark Warren that entirely engulfed me in fear and anguish.

"Not to worry, Bianca is in the car waiting for me."

'Why did I say that?' If he insisted on following me to my car, he would instantly know I was lying which in turn, would create suspicion of me.

"Alright. I'll call you tomorrow."

He walked up to me and kissed me gently. I felt repelled to my stomach, but I mustered up every little bit of courage inside of me and kissed him back. Until I knew what was going on with him and what his intentions were, I had to play his game. *Flawlessly.*

When I reached my car, I was frantic to leave the precinct and put as much distance between Mark and I as I possibly could. I didn't know where to go. I didn't know who to reach out to. I didn't really know any lawyers or attorneys in Willow County, and I didn't want to wake Bianca. After driving around aimlessly for almost an hour, I instinctively pulled up at the mall. I felt trapped in a storm with winds that were continually howling around me. I just wanted to sit for a while, and rest.

With my hands pressed against my ears, I tried to block out the screams that were escaping from my mouth, instead, I heard them growing louder and louder.

'This is all my fault.'

I despised Michael, but he didn't deserve to spend a single day in prison for a crime he did not commit. He didn't deserve to be accused of something he didn't do or be framed for something he would never do.

I slowly climbed out of my car and walked into the mall. It was quiet and deserted and just after four in the morning. I had to see Daniel. I needed his help, but how would I tell him that Mark had hidden his true self from me, like a snake covered with leaves. There was never an indication of evil intent or a hint of self-deviant motives.

His passion was his power over me. He knew my fears and understood what made me tick. He found a way to dangle an illusion in front of me and in the process, he became my worst nightmare.

'How do I tell Daniel that?'

Alice VL

When the elevator reached the sixth floor, I slowly walked out and cautiously walked up to Daniel's apartment. I should have called first, but I was afraid that I would lose my nerve.

'Shit.'

I stood at his door and took my mobile phone from my bag. My hands were shaking, my heart was pounding, and I wasn't sure what I'd find on the other side of those walls. I slowly dialed his number and waited. From the hallway, I could hear Daniel's phone ring.

"Ally?"

I didn't know what to say. Before I could say anything, I swallowed back on a lump in my throat, desperate to stop the tears from reaching my eyes.

As out of nowhere, the tears burst from my eyes, spilling down my face. My bottom lip shook as I trembled like a small child. I could hear my own sounds and it stole the last bit of dignity I thought I had left.

"Ally? Are you there? Say something!"

Alice VL

I DO (NOT) – ABOVE THE LAW

I swallowed again. It was as though the walls around me were collapsing onto me. I pressed my hand against his door and stood trembling in silence.

"I'm here … please let me in."

My voice was breaking. My heart was hammering, and my legs were shaking. Daniel opened his front door seconds later and when I saw him standing there in nothing but a pair of boxer shorts, I collapsed into his arms, defeated by the tears that were bucketing from my eyes.

I knew what I looked like. I had never learned to cry with style or silently. I wished I had. I wished I could hold it back, instead, the pain inside of me came out like an uproar from my throat.

"What's going on?"

He promptly pulled me inside and shut his front door behind me. He held me firmly in his arms and gently stroked my hair. He felt like home. He smelled like forest, wood and rain. I felt safe. Shielded. Loved. I felt *loved*.

I stepped back and hurriedly swabbed the tears from my cheeks. The more I dabbed at them, the stronger they gushed down my cheeks. Daniel did not once look away from me. His dark lashes unanticipatedly brimmed against a glisten in his eyes. He blinked suddenly, still unable to take his eyes off me. From where I was standing, I could have sworn that Daniel felt every raw emotion that was radiating from me.

"Is Lucy asleep?"

He placed his hands on my shoulders, and stared at me,

"She doesn't *live* here, Ally. She's not here."

I was instantly relieved. I didn't want to deal with Lucy or have to explain my presence to her. Daniel took me by my hand and led me into his living room. I sat on a couch before he sat down beside me. When the tears finally began to subside, I looked up at him,

"I'm so sorry for coming here this time of the night. I just didn't know where else to go?"

"What happened Ally?"

"Michael and Lily have been arrested and I think Mark set them up."

"Arrested? For what?"

"Arson and drug possession."

"Arson and drug possession? Wow."

I DO (NOT) – ABOVE THE LAW

"Michael is a douche, Daniel, but he isn't an arsonist or a drug dealer or user. I swear it. Nor is Lily."

"What grounds does he have to charge them?"

"An eye-witness apparently picked Michael as the arsonist from a line-up and when they served a warrant on their place, they found drugs. Michael says Mark planted it and framed him."

"Why would he do that? He's an officer of the law?"

I bowed my head. *'It's because of me.'* I knew it was, still, I didn't want Daniel to know. I didn't want to tell him the truth.

Daniel stood up at once and placed his hands on his head,

"You're screwing him?"

I nodded as the tears began to stream from my eyes once more.

"Fuck, Ally!"

What could I say? What could I do? When I looked up at Daniel, I was thrown by the look of disgust in his eyes. He looked at me as though I was swimming in filth and each time I was invited in, I jumped in thoughtlessly.

Alice VL

I DO (NOT) – ABOVE THE LAW

I got it all wrong, I knew that. I was no saint, but I did have integrity and honor, even though it didn't seem like it at that very moment. I just wanted *him* to see that.

Daniel turned and walked out of the living room. I covered my face with my hands and surrendered to the tears that were relentlessly overwhelming me. Barely a minute later, he walked back in with a T-shirt on.

"I know an attorney. I'll call him and see if he can see us on a Saturday. The first thing to do now is to get legal advice. If he can see us, we'll know what to do next."

Us. We.

I was so sure he was going to kick me out. Instead, he offered me an *us* and a *we*.

Daniel sat down beside me and placed an arm around me.

"Get some sleep. We can't do much until morning."

He stood up and held a hand out to me. I got up and placed my hand in his.

He led me into his bedroom and lifted the covers for me. I sat down and took off my sneakers and coat before I slithered into his bed. *'I don't deserve him.'*

Alice VL

Daniel slid the covers over me and took a throw from the end of his bed, before he made his way over to a chair in the corner.

"Daniel?"

"I'll be fine here …"

"I want you to hold me …"

He turned around and stood motionlessly for a moment before he walked over to his bed and slid in behind me. When he held me close against him, there was nowhere else I wanted to be. There was no-one's arms I wanted around me. He felt like home. He smelled like Heaven. Why couldn't I commit to this fireman?

'No, Ally. No.'

I closed my eyes, drunk on Daniel's highly addictive scent. His arms felt like a shield around me, a great piece of protective armor that was keeping me warm and comforted. I felt safe listening to his beating heart as he fell asleep.

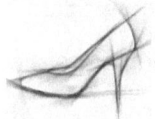

Alice VL

When I opened my eyes, it felt as though I had been asleep for hours. Glancing over at a clock on the wall, it was but a few minutes after seven. I turned around slowly, careful not to wake him.

Daniel was laying snugly against me, breathing softly but firmly holding me. For the first time since I had met Daniel, I noticed how his features were much subtler when he was asleep. I trailed the lines that usually creased his brow but that were replaced by a more youthful appearance while he lay sleeping.

Serenity was plastered across his face as he slept. Peacefully. *Quietly.* He was almost too quiet was it not for slight movements with each rise and fall of his chest.

I wanted to lay still and absorb Daniel and the warmth emanating from his skin. I wanted to smell him before he awakes and savor all there was about Daniel.

When he pulled me tightly against him, I knew he was still fast asleep. There was nothing more attractive about Daniel, than having him pull me closer to him in his sleep. Was he thinking of Lucy? I didn't know. I didn't *care.* I was there and Lucy *woozy* wasn't. He was holding me, not *her.* There was only one thing on my mind. His skin on mine. I felt him stir slightly against me and couldn't help but notice again how perfect our bodies fit together. It felt familiar. *Right.*

Absorbing the natural rhythm his body was making, I smiled as he again stirred slightly. With nothing else on my mind; no Mark and no Michael, I gently trailed his body with my fingers as gently as I possibly could. Daniel muttered softly,

"Ally."

'Yes. It's me, Ally.'

Hearing him say my name like that sent gentle thumps through my heart. Like a slow, soft tango dancing into the light without a single note from an orchestra. For a second, I didn't want to move or breathe as the hairs on my arms stood up straight.

I shifted out from under his arm, and when he turned on his back, I lowered the covers, and gently slid onto him. Daniel Sotherby was like a little frosting from Heaven. There was something exceptional and extraordinary about him, and every inch of his body showed no traces of flaws or quirks.

I *knew* him. I *craved* him.

He was instantly wide awake and when I kissed him, he again, felt like home. I glanced over at him and met his gaze.

Alice VL

Daniel placed his arms around me and began squirming softly as he lifted himself slightly. There was something so sensual and vulnerable about Daniel. I wanted him to remember me. I wanted him to think of *me* each time he looked at Lucy. *I wanted Daniel Sotherby to fight for me.*

A second later, I could feel a million tiny pulses throbbing from him, like tiny ripples under his skin. Daniel placed both his hands around my head and pushed his lips against mine with force.

"Fuck, Ally."

His voice was warm and rich. My heart beat faster when he stared at me, waiting for a response. Instead of saying anything, I blushed, and his look of bafflement turned into an inhibited smile.

In one motion, he turned me onto my back and kissed me with a mouth that fit perfectly on mine. His was the only tongue that intertwined so flawlessly with mine.

"Ally"

Never had my name ever sounded so wonderful. His hand rested below my ear as his thumb caressed my cheeks. I ran my fingers down his spine, pulling him closer to me.

I closed my eyes and savored every bit of him against me, keenly aware of my racing heart and shuddering hands. With my arms around him, I held him firmly and kissed him more passionately. I didn't want Daniel to give up on me. I didn't want him to forget me. I *needed* him. I *wanted* him. I just didn't want to tell him *at that moment*.

He pressed himself firmly onto me and when he slid his arms in under me, I cringed. My back arched spontaneously and my mouth opened slightly. He stopped kissing me, yet, he kept his lips pressed against mine.

He moved slowly and gently. Tenderly. It felt like *love*. I opened my eyes, and when my eyes locked into his, I could see a million reasons to love him, yet, I couldn't recognize an entitlement to his love in there.

Was it love, or was it lust? Was it our passion bonding us together? *I didn't know*? I couldn't tell. All I knew was that when I was away from Daniel, there was a hole, and an excruciating emptiness inside of me. Without taking my eyes off him, I savored each sensation that was beginning to wake up and respond to Daniel in every way.

He was my obsession. He was who I was besotted with. As though my entire body had ordered and scheduled one single, orgasmic explosion, it obeyed dutifully, and burst from the very core of me.

My eyes rolled back slightly as I desperately tried to keep his gaze. My breathing was irregular and strained. Daniel stared at me as his breathing became shorter and brisker.

I dug my fingers into him, desperate to keep my eyes on his. He lifted me slightly, still holding tightly onto me. My back arched again as each and every pressure point was activated and exploded. There was no feeling, no comparison and no way in the world to explain the summit Daniel took me to.

Again, I had a quaint feeling that there would never be a comparable sexual pleasure, like the decadence Daniel so effortlessly handed to me. As his body enthusiastically constricted and intensified, I ran my hands down to the small of his back and pressed him down on me. He buried his head in my neck and shuddered in my arms for just a moment.

Almost a second later, he was still. His breathing was loud but fleeting. While he lay quietly, I buried my face in his hair and smelled him into my soul. There was nowhere else I would rather have been, than under Daniel Sotherby. He lifted somewhat and smiled,

"What are we doing?"

Alice VL

"What we said we would …" I didn't want Daniel to regret a moment I knew I would never forget.

"God, Ally."

He rolled off and peered over at me. Like a video camera, his eyes captured my entire body and when they reached my thighs, he frowned before he shot an angry stare at me. Somehow I knew that the moment was lost.

"What the fuck, Ally?

'What?' I glowered at him, unsure of where his sudden anger had come from.

"What?"

I whispered hoarsely as he inadvertently clenched his fists and gritted his teeth. I knew when his face instantly mottled, that he was suppressing a kind of rage I too, had never seen before. I had no clue why or where it suddenly came from?

"What the fuck is *that*?"

He pointed to my thighs, as though I was covered in a deathly poison. I sat up straight and glanced down. 'Shit.' There were a cluster of bruises on both my inner and outer thighs from Mark's tight grip in the precinct only days before.

I laid down instantly and had no inkling of what to say or how to explain away the bruises. Daniel suddenly appeared to be like a volcano about to erupt into a fury that would sweep off me like ferocious waves. There was a look of wrath that consumed me and engulfed my moralities while destroying any boundary of loyalty that was left between us.

'I blew it.'

"It's him, isn't it?"

I looked away. The disappointment in his voice caught me unexpectedly off-guard. I couldn't imagine the expression in his eyes, and I didn't want to see it.

"This is what you look like after screwing him?"

When he raised his voice, I knew that his patience was wearing thin and that he had reached breaking point. I didn't blame him, even though his words were packing a powerful punch to my heart.

I turned to face him and knew instantly by the look in his eyes that we had hit our mark. I had somehow managed to shatter what I had with Daniel, into a million glassy shards. Nothing would ever be the same again. I had spoilt our moment.

I DO (NOT) – ABOVE THE LAW

I had missed what could have been illustrious, and it was my own fault.

Daniel got up without saying another word, and quickly made his way into his bathroom. I laid quietly and when he turned the shower taps on, I tiptoed over to him and snuck in behind him. I didn't want to lose Daniel, yet, I didn't know how to take back what he had seen only seconds before.

"Really, Ally?"

I was no good at apologizing, *ever*. I didn't know what to say. I had failed not only Daniel, but I had failed myself too. I had believed my entire life that love was a possession and that all I wanted was to be free from it. I hurt Daniel. I knew from the bottom of my heart that I had crushed his spirit. My heart wanted to retract all that I had done to him, only, my voice wouldn't let me say it.

With a misplaced sense of entitlement towards Daniel, I became so absorbed with my own needs, that I pushed him away. I let him down and ignorantly, taunted him with his own failures. I was remorseful.

"I just want to shower ..." I wanted to pretend that Daniel never saw the traces of another man on my body.

"Ally ... I am mad as hell at you."

I took a step closer to him. Even though I still didn't know what to say to him, at the very least, I wanted to try.

"I know, Danny. I am no good at this. I am terrible at all of this. I am still learning, just please ... don't turn your back on me now ..."

Daniel lowered his head, and took my hands into his,

"Please Danny ... I am trying to figure things out ... but right now, I need a shower and I want one with *you*."

He chuckled and shook his head when I took the bar of soap from him, and quickly sponged myself down. I wanted to rather ask for forgiveness, than permission. I didn't want to lose Daniel. I didn't want him to give up on me; I just didn't know how to ask him.

"One of these days, Ally Bradshaw, you're going to realize that you should never have let me slip through your fingers."

He said it as though he had decided. *It hit me hard.* His words were like nails and hammers breaking my heart into a million pieces.

'I can't lose Daniel.'

Alice VL

I DO (NOT) – ABOVE THE LAW

There was no way I could stand in the shower with him for a minute longer, and when I slipped out, I hurriedly dressed back into my clothes from the previous night. Only a moment later, did Daniel stroll into his bedroom with nothing but a towel around him. I stared shamelessly. I gazed at him, suddenly defeated and crippled by the sorrow and wretchedness that had crept up on me. *I was hurt.*

He quickly slipped on a pair of ripped jeans, a white T-Shirt and a brand-new pair of sneakers. After he had brushed his hair, he quickly slapped cologne on. '*Aah.*' His scent. Daniel brushed past me and smiled before I followed him into the kitchen where he poured us each a cup of coffee.

An eerie silence suddenly surrounded us as we sat sipping on our coffee. It felt as though there was an unexpected, but slight drop in the temperature which led to the descent of absolute silence.

I looked at him often. I couldn't quite decide what I was seeing in Daniel, but I was sure it was a combination of anger, sadness, rage, betrayal, disgust and hurt.

I felt ashamed. I had betrayed him, even though I didn't *really*. I hurt him. He hurt me. He *was* hurting me at that very moment. I never set out to fall in love with Daniel, and I was not even sure I did, but whatever I was feeling; it felt as though it was slowly and mercilessly killing me.

That was never the plan in the grand scheme of what was supposed to be the newly-single Ally Bradshaw. Falling in love was never what I wanted. I was not ready to give my heart away again and to be honest, I thought I never *would*. There was not one single moment since my divorce from Michael that I saw the warning signs, or thought it was even possible.

Except, without me noticing or paying much attention to my heart, Daniel snuck in and was now stuck there, deep inside of me somewhere. *It hurt.* When there was a startling knock on his front door, I was instantly yanked back to reality and enormously relieved.

"Shit."

"What?"

"It's Lucy ..."

'Oh Lawd.'

Daniel hurriedly made his way over to the front door and when he opened it for Lucy, she instantly flung her arms around him.

"I couldn't wait to see you!"

I DO (NOT) – ABOVE THE LAW

"Come on into the kitchen. We're having coffee."

"We?"

When Lucy walked in, the disappointment on her face was unmistakable. Even though her feelings weren't visible, there was a vibe about her that made me understand in no uncertain terms that I was invading her space and overstaying my welcome in Daniel's life.

She shot a dagger-filled glare at me, before she summoned a forced smile.

"Yeah, Ally stopped by. I'm taking her to see Damon Kingston later. Long story."

"Oh. Okay."

"Hi Lucy. Nice to see you again."

'*Bitch.*' I could feel claws replacing my finger nails just by looking at her. Lucy was dressed in a tight-fitting pair of skinny jeans that I knew, I would never be able to climb into even though I jumped into them from the sixteenth floor of Daniel's building.

Her hair was beautifully curled and her make-up was flawlessly applied. I was making an effort to see only the good in her, but all I really wanted was to tell her that I had just spent the night with her man.

Alice VL

'Stop, Ally. Remember Michael and Lily? Remember how they made you feel? Whatever.'

I retracted my invisible claws at once and turned away from her. I felt a little shamefaced for spending the night with her man. *No, I didn't.* Nevertheless, I couldn't look her in the eye afterwards, and carried on sipping my coffee in an awkward silence.

'I should call Bianca and let her know about Michael. Later.'

"So, my dad's invited us to the lake house today. I thought we could spend the night and come back to the city tomorrow?"

Daniel sighed and looked at me, before he glanced back at her. I immediately lowered my head and pretended not to hear.

"I'm on stand-by. I can't leave especially with all the arson attacks. Maybe next time?"

'Liar.'

"Okay. Do you mind if I go?"

"Not at all. Have fun."

Alice VL

I DO (NOT) – ABOVE THE LAW

Daniel sounded just a tad bit too eager to send Lucy out of town for the next two days. I *liked* it. Lucy shot a glance my way and as though a sudden and unanticipated light bulb lit up above her head or inside of her somewhere, she at once backtracked and discarded her initial decision.

With her arms around Daniel, I noticed the sudden hesitation and fear in her eyes. *Right then*, I felt honest pity for her.

"You know what? I can always go later when you're not working ..."

"I don't mind, Lucy ... you should go."

"No, I'd rather spend it with you doing absolutely nothing at all."

'Nope. She's still a bitch.'

Alice VL

I DO (NOT) – ABOVE THE LAW

PART 5

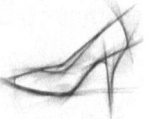

Daniel, Lucy and I walked into the offices of Damon Kingston shortly after ten that same morning when he agreed to meet us at his offices in town.

Michael and Lily did in no way at all deserve to spend the weekend in jail especially since I had a strong feeling that they were there because of me. *Because of Mark.* Because I told Mark that Michael wanted me back, and that he was incessantly harassing me.

I didn't *want* to believe that Mark had set them both up, but at the same time, I had no other explanation for the supposed eye witness or the narcotics found in their home.

The three of us sat quietly in the waiting room, and when Damon Kingston appeared from his office, I was instantly thrown by his appearance. *I know, that happens a lot lately.* It was almost as though I was seeing all these men for the very first time.

I honestly expected an older, balding man with a protruding belly who had at least thirty years of *lawyering* behind him. *'Lawyering? I honestly must stop conjuring up words that don't exist.'*

Instead, a man I assumed to be in his early forties, with pitch black hair and almost darker eyes stood before us. I guessed him to be Daniel's length, but slimmer, although not scrawny. *Not Michael scrawny.* His suit shouted elegance, style and wealth; his shoes were probably worth my apartment and all my belongings in the entire world. Probably my parents' farm too.

"Hey Dan ..."

Daniel stood up at once and shook Damon's hand.

"Thanks for seeing us today ..."

"No problem. Always happy to help a friend out."

Daniel turned to me and held out his hand. I got up and quickly made my way over to them. I was feeling a little self-conscious and conquered by his impression of supremacy.

"You must be Ally Bradshaw?"

He took my hand and gently shook it. Soft. Silky. *But firm.*

'Oh Lord. There it goes again.' My leg lifted slightly behind me and I began swinging marginally, but noticeably. *'How did I never notice these men in Willow County before?'*

Alice VL

*'None so blind as those who don't want to see, Ally.
Whatever.'* I was seeing just fine while standing in front of Damon
Kingston, and introduced to a whiff I couldn't quite place.
Definitely musky but I couldn't for the life of me, figure out an
added, deeply overpowering scent. Maybe, it was just *him*?

The animal in me began absorbing the overwhelming
scent that not only attracted me to him like honey does to bees,
but that made my pleasure senses pulsate.

"Pleased to meet you, Mr. Kingston. Thank you for seeing
me."

"It really is no problem. You can come through to my
office…"

Daniel glared at me and when I noticed the poignant look
in his eyes, I stopped swinging and pulled myself together at
once. Damon turned to lead us into his office and before Daniel
closed the door behind him, he peered over at Lucy,

"This shouldn't take too long."

"No worries, baby."

'Aah. That word again. Baby. Bitch.'

Daniel pulled up a seat next to me, while Damon slid into
an expensive leather chair behind an equally pricy Rosewood

desk. He quickly pulled out a notepad and picked up an equally expensive looking pen.

I glanced around his office and was pleasantly swept up by his furniture and finishings. There was nothing cheap about this office; there was nothing artificial about Damon Kingston, and I kind of felt a little seduced by it all. *Not that I ever was that kind of person.* From where I was sitting, there was no mistaking that he wore only the finest designer clothes that coordinated with his office. His hair was expertly cut and by the way he spoke, there was no denying his upper class education.

"So, Miss Bradshaw ..."

"Ally. Just Ally."

I smiled and from the corner of my eye, I could feel Daniel's eyes on me.

"Daniel said something about your ex-husband and his fiancée arrested last night for drug possession and arson?"

I cringed. I knew into the very core of me that Michael was not capable of the crimes he was being accused of. He was a dick, but he was a straight-shooting dick.

"There has been a spate of arson cases in the last few months and we have reason to believe that it's a local gang, possibly part of an initiation routine. I highly doubt any of the fires set were by Michael Bradshaw."

Daniel interrupted before I could voice my own concerns.

"He isn't capable of that, Mr. Kingston. I don't know where that eye witness came from, but he's wrong."

"You can just call me Damon."

I grinned from ear to ear. We were on a first-name basis and *I liked that.*

"And as far as the drug possession charges goes, Michael swears that Detective Mark Warren planted it in his apartment the same night they served the warrant on him."

Damon looked up and frowned. By the expression on his face it was clear that Damon Kingston had perfected the art of argument in legalistic language which more than likely commanded exorbitant fees.

"Mark Warren? Detective Mark Warren? Are you sure he was the arresting officer?"

"Yes. I mean, I can't say for sure that he planted the drugs, but he made the arrest."

Damon placed his pen down and leaned back into his chair. Again, I was distracted by his appearance and couldn't help but wonder what he looked like behind his tailor-made suit. His skin was perfect, his teeth were flawless and there was not a hair out of place.

"Well, this changes everything." He suddenly leaned forward and rested his elbows on his desk.

"What do you mean?"

Daniel mimicked him and leaned forward, placing his own elbows on Damon's highly expensive, shiny desk.

"Can I ask you a personal question?"

Damon was glaring questioningly at me, before Daniel turned to face me. I suddenly felt ganged-up on and had no clue why.

"Yes?"

"Is there anything going on between you and Detective Warren?"

I could feel the blood first drain my face, before it rushed back when my heart almost missed a beat. I didn't want to tell him about Mark in front of Daniel. I could feel Daniel's eyes on me, before he turned away and lowered his head. I knew what he was thinking.

"No. Well … casual … I mean, it's not a relationship. We don't have a relationship … really …"

"God Ally, just tell him you are sleeping with him."

Daniel's agitation threw me off-guard. I was mortified, but more than that, I was unnerved by his sudden anger.

I had never felt as embarrassed and humiliated as I did at that very moment. Daniel blurting out my not-so-secret encounters with Mark was something I never expected or thought he would do. I bowed my head and fidgeted. I could hardly look either of them in the eye.

"Okay. Well, that's all I needed to know. Will you two excuse me for a second?"

"Sure."

Daniel sat back and folded his legs.

"That was uncalled for, Daniel."

"Why? It's the truth and if you want Damon to help Michael and Lily, you have to come clean about your relationship with Mark."

"It's not a relationship. And besides, did you have to say it like that?"

"How should I have said it? You're sleeping with him, and I just had to look at your thighs to see how hard he really fucked you."

I felt the tears well up inside of me. I was offended, belittled and suddenly, I felt like the queen of a dollar note again.

Daniel placed his hand on mine, almost as though he was apologizing. As though, he immediately regretted the harsh words that came out, lashing at me. But in all honesty, Daniel's anger was simply a reflection of my own inner demons.

"Ally, what happened between us this morning, it shouldn't have. I am sorry. I should have stopped. I am trying really hard to give this thing with Lucy a chance, and I want you to let me. I want you to respect that and give me that chance with her. I know there is something worth trying for with Lily and ... I want to try."

"I know you do. I missed my chance, didn't I?"

"Yeah, you did, Ally. But, I care so much, and I hope we can find a way to move forward and just be the friends we set out to be?"

I DO (NOT) – ABOVE THE LAW

"I know, Danny. I can try, I just can't if you're going to be mad at me all the time. You're throwing punches at me the moment the opportunity presents itself."

He squeezed my hand, and leaned closer to me,

"I am sorry. It just hurts. Knowing Mark is screwing you, and possibly a cowboy before him … it hurts, Ally. You don't owe me anything … but, it still gets to me and that is why I so badly want to make things work with Lucy."

"I'm sorry too … but more than anything, Danny … I'm sorry I hurt you."

The moment grew unnervingly intense that by the time Damon walked in, I breathed an enormous sigh of relief. Daniel's words cut deeper than I ever thought it could. Damon quickly made his way around his desk before he slid back into his chair.

I felt like crying. Daniel had me flustered and heartbroken. I was devastated. He was falling in love with Lucy. He was falling out of love with me and desperately trying to fall in love with her.

"So, I've just spoken to a contact on another case of mine which also involves Detective Mark Warren. You may not know this, but he's been the target of an investigation by Internal Affairs for months now."

I gasped for air. Daniel glowered before he gazed over at me.

"I can only set a bail hearing for Monday morning. There is no judge that is prepared to grant bail today, and my buddy, Judge Chandler is away for the weekend. In the meantime, do you think you can get him to confess to planting the drugs, Ally?"

"To framing Michael?" I hesitated for a moment, "I mean, I can try ..."

"I only need him to confess to planting the drugs. If you can do that, we can get the other charges against your ex-husband and his fiancée dropped before Monday."

"So then, you *do* think he planted the drugs?"

"I do."

"How would I go about doing that? How would I get him to confess and get *proof* of his confession?"

"We'll place a listening device on your mobile phone. Try to get him to admit to framing Michael and why he did it. If we can get that, all charges against Michael and Lily will be dropped and we can work on the so-called witness in the arson case. He will lose all credibility anyway, so there shouldn't even be a hearing."

Daniel sat up straight,

"No. She's not going to place herself in that position with Mark. He is dangerous Damon, and if he thinks she's working against him, who knows what he'll do to her? We don't know what he's capable of."

"We'll be close by. I have two undercovers who won't let her out of their sight. It's the only chance we've got to get her ex-husband out before Monday."

"I'm sorry, I'm not going to let her do that."

My heart smiled for the first time since we left Daniel's apartment. I placed my hand on his leg, and squeezed it gently,

"I owe them this, Danny. It's my fault they're in jail. I have to do this."

"You are not doing this, Ally. Look at the bruises on your body."

I bowed my head again. And again, I was ashamed. Damon turned back to his notepad and pretended not to hear. *'Was that necessary?'*

Alice VL

"Daniel, I can handle it. I'll be fine, and you heard what Damon said; I won't be alone."

Daniel shook his head and placed his hand over mine before he turned back to Damon Kingston,

"Then I want to be there too. You are gonna have to get me in there somehow."

Damon nodded in agreement before he dialed a number from his mobile,

"Okay. Let's do this."

When he ended the call, he turned back to me,

"Agents Smith and Jackson are on their way. They'll fit your phone with the device and coach you into getting a confession. In the meantime, while we wait, call Detective Warren and arrange a meeting with him for tonight."

My hands began shaking. I was nervous and suddenly, deathly afraid of Mark Warren. I slowly dialed his number and when he answered, I couldn't quite believe that his voice matched that of a dirty cop,

"Hello sexy."

"Hey ..."

I DO (NOT) – ABOVE THE LAW

"You okay?"

"Yes, fine. No worries. So … I wanted to know if you'd like to join me for dinner tonight?"

"Yeah … sounds good. What did you have in mind?"

I didn't want him at my apartment, and I was not prepared to meet him at his place.

"The Red Velvet?"

Daniel glared at me before he lowered his head and shook it. I couldn't think of one other restaurant but The Red Velvet; the same restaurant that Daniel and I had our very first, and very last date at. It was the only intimate, but public place I could think of.

"Alright. What time?"

"Nine'ish?"

"Good. I'll see you then."

It suddenly bothered me that he did not offer to pick me up, there was *nothing*. Just *'I'll see you then.'* That alone told me in no uncertain terms exactly how detached Mark Warren was, and how un-gentlemanly he is. *Un-gentlemanly?*

"Bye."

Alice VL

I ended the call at once, aware of the sudden quiver in my voice. Damon nodded before he got up and walked out again.

"Really, Ally? The Red Velvet?"

"I couldn't think of another place."

"Right."

"I'm sorry, Daniel. I am scared to death of this man, and all you can think of is that I picked the restaurant you and I went to?"

"It's the little things, Ally. And yes, it's a little unnerving. I don't want you to do this."

"I have to Daniel. I can't let Michael go to prison for something he didn't do."

"I know."

"Please, why don't you go home with Lucy? I don't want you in the middle of all of this. I'll be fine, you'll see."

"Shit, speaking of. Let's not tell Lucy about any of this. I'll just tell her I'm working; that I've been called in for shift."

"Okay."

There was no way in the world that Daniel was not going to be close by when I met with Mark. He was having nothing of it and again, my heart smiled. When Damon walked back in, he was followed in by two men that looked as though he had picked them up out of a gutter.

They were both dressed in shabby, patched clothes, none of it that matched, and battered looking. One of them were wearing corduroy trousers and a checked shirt while the other wore baggy jeans and a shirt missing buttons.

I would never have guessed that these two men who were disguised as the homeless, were in fact, undercover officers.

"Ally, this is Jack Smith and Donny Jackson. They will get you ready and set up for tonight.

"How do you do, ma'am?"

"Hi."

Donny Jackson smiled and placed a hand on my shoulder,

"We won't let anything happen to you. You're in good hands."

"Right then. Give Jack your mobile phone and I'll take you through the plan."

Alice VL

"Okay."

I got up and handed my phone over to Jack Smith. When Donny made his way back to me, Daniel got up from his chair and joined us.

"So, you are going to meet Detective Warren as though we're not even there. Like, it's just another normal evening out with your man. Don't push him and don't try and get too much information too quickly. We have the whole night. Don't, under any circumstances leave the restaurant with him, no matter what."

"Okay."

"Where will you be?" Daniel's voice was shaky.

His mind was clearly racing as he listened intently to Donny Jackson walking me through the plans for the evening.

"Jack and another undercover officer will be in the restaurant like any other normal couple, while I'll be outside listening."

"Right, so that's where I'll be."

"I said Daniel could tag along." Damon interrupted before Donny could object.

Once the phone was fitted with a listening and recording device, Jack Smith assured me that they would be at the restaurant by the time I arrived and that they would have ears on our entire conversation.

When they left, Daniel placed both his hands on my shoulders,

"It'll be fine. I'll be there too. The moment things aren't right, we'll get you out of there."

"Okay. Thank you."

He smiled, desperate to calm and reassure me, and when I noticed the expression on his face, it felt again as though Daniel had sent the sun to shine just for me.

When Daniel and I walked out, Lucy quickly rose to her feet and grabbed Daniel's hand.

"Everything alright?"

"Yep. Everything's good."

"Good."

Lucy frowned and shot another sharp, fiery but invisible dagger over at me.

"How about breakfast?"

Alice VL

"Ally's car is at the apartment ... she needs to get home. Besides, I have to work later ... can we reschedule?"

"Sure. When were you called into work?

"Oh ... while we were in there."

"Alright."

I walked out ahead of them. Lucy *woozy* was irritating the shit out of me and asking too many questions, almost as though she *owned* Daniel. She was almost too perfect, too sweet and too concerned about Daniel. *She was onto me.*

On our drive back to Daniel's apartment, I couldn't help but sneak in glimpses at him through the rearview mirror. Each time I would look up, Daniel would be looking back at me.

Was he simply just concerned for my safety? Or, was there something more in Daniel's eyes? I couldn't tell, especially after our conversation in Damon's office.

Lucy had her hand firmly planted on his leg and would engage in lighthearted chatter with him. From the expression on Daniel's face, I knew he wasn't listening to a word she was saying.

When we finally reached his apartment, I was eager to get home immediately. I wanted to get away from perfect Miss Lucy and away from Daniel.

Alice VL

I DO (NOT) – ABOVE THE LAW

"So, thanks for taking me …"

"You can't go *now* …"

Daniel whispered in my ear as Lucy climbed out of his car.

"I'm not letting you go home alone."

"What am I supposed to do?"

I whispered back when it became obvious that he didn't want Lucy to hear us. When Lucy joined us, Daniel smiled at her,

"So, I'll see you tomorrow? We can go out for a movie if you like?"

"You have to be at work *now*?"

"Yep. I am late actually."

"Alright. Call me later?"

Daniel bent down and kissed her gently on her lips. *Bitch*. I once again failed to explain the emotions that were slowly, but wholly submerging me. Rejection was tough. It didn't feel good and it stung. I was learning just how much it hurt, and slowly discovered how I made Daniel feel. Perhaps, it was how I made them all feel. It was almost like a germ growing inside of me, ready to choke out all the hope my heart had. One, I didn't expect or hope for, and one, I never thought I *wanted*.

Alice VL

When Lucy reached her car, she turned back and waved at Daniel. She came across as worried and tensed, and I honestly couldn't blame her. I was an awful person. On one hand, I felt guilty, but on the other, I *didn't.* I quickly turned around and marched over to my parked car. I had hardly reached my car when Daniel caught up with me.

"I'll follow you home …"

"You don't have to babysit me, Daniel."

"Actually, I do. You and I both know that you can't be there alone … what if Mark catches a whiff of what you're up to?"

When I climbed in behind the wheel, Daniel turned around and made a frantic dash for his truck. I pulled out of my parking spot, and when I glanced back in the rearview mirror, he was right behind me.

Alice VL

I nervously unlocked my apartment, and quickly made my way into the kitchen. Daniel locked my front door behind him and followed me inside.

"This is nice." He glanced around my apartment while following me into the kitchen.

"Thanks."

He had never been there before. Not once did I ever invite him to my home. Glancing over at Daniel, I once again berated myself for letting him slip through my fingers.

"I have croissants and coffee?"

"Yep. That would be great."

Daniel seemed distracted and withdrawn. I peered over at him often and couldn't disregard the uncertainty and worry in his eyes. His mind kept wandering off to somewhere I had no clue where to. The look in his eyes was distant more often than I would care to admit, and yet, I was at the center of it all.

We ate croissants and drank coffee in silence. I suddenly didn't know what to say to him; there was nothing at all that came to mind. Perhaps, we were both just preoccupied with the events that would inevitably unfold in a few hours, or perhaps, I had plunged the final nail into what *could have been.*

Alice VL

"Do you fancy a movie? We can't just sit here and do nothing all day." I had to say something.

"Sure, why not?"

Once we were in the living room, I quickly turned on the television and handed Daniel the remote control. I was too distracted to focus on anything and thought Daniel might be able to pass the time by flicking through the channels.

When he found something that I thought would hopefully entertain him for a few hours, he placed the remote control onto a coffee table. I chuckled softly when I recognized a golden oldie, 'Gone with the wind.' Daniel never failed to surprise me.

I sat down beside him in silence. I was determined to get my mind off Mark and sit through a painful black and white screening of Scarlet O'Hara with Daniel, who clearly found pleasure in old love stories.

It was getting colder and when I opened my eyes, I was surprised to discover that I had fallen asleep on Daniel's shoulder. When I gazed over at him, he had rested his head back against my couch, and had fallen asleep too. I stared at him for a moment. What a fool I was. Daniel Sotherby was the real deal. *Authentic*. Gorgeous. Hard-working. Caring. But more than anything, he was sensual at a level I could not yet compare another man to. I was tempted to kiss his inviting lips and stroke his flustered cheeks.

I stirred slightly, not wanting to wake him, but when he opened his eyes, I realized again how jumpy he was. His eyes were instantly searing for a sign that I was alright. My stomach shifted uneasily. I hated seeing him restless and jittery.

"You okay?"

"Yes. Sorry, I didn't want to wake you."

He leaned back again and pulled me closer. I rested my head on his chest and when I heard his heartbeat, I so desperately wanted to be home in his heart.

His scent, mixed in with his beautiful, perfect heartbeat entirely conquered me. I looked up and when he looked down, his lips were magnetically drawn to mine.

I closed my eyes and tasted his mouth. Daniel kissed me overpoweringly and held me firmly against him. I turned and climbed onto his lap before I lowered my head and kissed him again, clutching his head into my hands. There was nothing to say. Nothing to explain, and nothing to apologize for. Daniel was mine for the moment. For a brief moment in time, I escaped back into a world Daniel had created for me; for just the two of us. It was a place that brought my heart home, and offered me safety and love. It was somewhere in a world of dimensions reserved for only the two of us where nothing else mattered and no-one else belonged. It was where I wanted to run to, and live forever.

I pressed myself against him and when his arms folded around me, I knew that there was nothing more to fear. Daniel couldn't deny me, he *didn't*. He was beginning to shift awkwardly beneath me and when his hands trailed down to my hips, he pressed me firmly onto him.

My hands were frantic to reach his zipper. I wanted him against me and I wanted all of him to meet me in our world. I was caught in his web, and I didn't want to be let out.

Daniel lifted his hand and slowly flicked away the auburn wisps behind my ear. He was staring at me. I could feel his eyes burn on my skin as I frantically tugged at his zipper. There was nothing in his eyes commanding me to stop. There were no signs of insecurity or hesitation. I had just managed to unzip his jeans when there was a loud and urgent knock on my door,

"Shit." Daniel was breathing rapidly,

"You expecting anyone?"

Alice VL

"No."

I didn't want to stop and kissed him again. Again, there was another knock on my door. It couldn't be Michael, he was in jail. It wasn't Bianca, she called first. And then, almost out of nowhere, it hit me. *It was Mark.* It had to be.

"Shit. It can only be Mark. You have to hide."

I jumped off Daniel and quickly straightened myself out. Fear suddenly gripped at my heart when I considered the fact that he might just lose his mind if he found Daniel in my apartment.

"The fire escape, outside my bedroom window."

Daniel made a frantic dash for my bedroom, before I slowly made my way to my front door. I stood still for a second and took in a deep breath of fresh air. When I opened the front door, Mark was standing on the other side, leaning against the wall.

"Hi ..."

"Hey ... this is a surprise. What are you doing here? Don't tell me you are standing me up tonight?" I could hear the shudder in my own voice and desperately prayed that he didn't.

Alice VL

I DO (NOT) – ABOVE THE LAW

His eyes were drilling into mine. They were soulless. Lifeless. There was no expression, only a bottomless pool of darkness and a kind of fierceness I could not ignore.

'He can't know, can he?'

"I wanted to see you …"

He brushed past me and peered into the living room. By the way he was searching through my apartment, I knew he was suspicious. My heart was racing at the speed of a freight train, desperate to keep the fear that settled into my veins away from my facial muscles and expressions.

"Watching a movie? All by yourself?"

"Yep, but I was just about to get ready for tonight …"

He walked into the kitchen and when he noticed the two coffee mugs and side plates in the basin, he frowned at once.

"Do you have company?"

"No?"

Mark Warren was one hell of a detective. The coffee mugs and side plates had given me away. I had to come up with something, and quickly.

"Bianca was here earlier …"

Alice VL

I DO (NOT) – ABOVE THE LAW

Without responding, he quickly made his way down the passage and into my bedroom. He glanced around and peered into my bathroom.

"What are you looking for?"

My stomach turned. My heart was about to thump right out of my chest. I didn't want to submit to the sudden anxiety that felt as though it would induce paralysis at any moment, but by the look on his face, I was introduced to a cage closing in around me, sealing off any viable exit. He walked over to me and placed a hand around my neck.

"You are mine, Ally Bradshaw. Do you know what I would do to any man that tries to take you away from me?"

I swallowed back on the lump that appeared almost out of nowhere. I was terrified. There was something in his eyes that reminded me of a wild animal. I couldn't breathe as his grip around me tightened. He was choking me.

"There's no-one else ... you're scaring me ..."

He released his hold on me and kissed me before he pressed himself against me. His hand grabbed a hold of my thighs before he looked me squarely in the eye,

"I don't know what I'd do if you ever cheated on me."

Alice VL

'Cheated on him? We're not even dating.'

He pushed me onto my bed and in one foul sweep, he ripped my blouse off me.

"Stop it Mark. What's wrong with you?"

"You just drive me so wild, Ally."

He placed his full weight on me and again, I could hardly breathe. When he pressed his lips against mine, it felt as though he was suffocating me. I closed my hands and landed my fists into his chest, desperate to push him off me, but he was too strong. I lifted my legs, but he only clenched his firmly around them. I couldn't move.

When I bit his lower lip, he retreated slightly and slapped me across my face. It stung, but more than that, I was shocked and stunned. From the corner of my eye, I could see Daniel about to climb back through my bedroom window.

'I had to do it now.' My phone was on the kitchen counter, but at the very least, Daniel could bear witness to his admission, if there was one.

"Is that why you planted the drugs in Michael's apartment? Because of me?"

Alice VL

Daniel stopped. Frozen. He pulled out his mobile phone, and after fidgeting for a second, he placed it on the window sill.

"I am not prepared to share my girl with any man?"

"But, he's marrying Lily. Why did you have to frame him, Mark?"

"To teach him a lesson Ally."

"What lesson? And what about Lily? What did she ever do?"

"What lesson? He wants you back and my girl is off-limits. And as far as Lily is concerned … well, there are always casualties in any good war. Sometimes, you have to sacrifice someone for the greater good."

"The greater good? And the fire at the museum? The witness?"

"There's no witness. No credible witness anyway. It's amazing what you can buy with drugs. Besides, it's probably just a local gang of youngsters causing havoc."

"Where did you get the drugs?"

"I own the streets, baby!"

Alice VL

Anger entirely overwhelmed me when I realized what Mark was capable of. I punched him and pushed him with all my might, desperate to get him off me.

"Oh no ... you're not going anywhere. He bent down and kissed me, while groping at my breasts."

"Get off me!"

I was frantic to get him off me, and when I turned my head towards the window, Daniel was standing next to me. He grabbed Mark off me and threw him to the ground.

"Fuck me. She's fucking you too?"

Daniel picked him up from the floor and punched him to the ground once again. There was blood everywhere. I jumped up and quickly tried to cover myself up after he had ripped my blouse off me. Mark stared at me before he burst out laughing,

"You, Ally Bradshaw, are one fucking cock teaser."

I gazed over at Daniel, who was ready to pack another punch. Mark wiped his nose, and when he saw the blood, he reached for his weapon.

"Danny!" Daniel in turn, reached for Mark's weapon too and struggled with him on the floor, for control of it. I was terrified. Horrified. I was deathly afraid that Daniel might be hurt.

Alice VL

I DO (NOT) – ABOVE THE LAW

When a shot went off, my heart just about came to a complete halt. It stopped dead. I froze and stared. I tried to make out whether anyone was shot, and when Mark burst out laughing again, I was so sure that Daniel was hit.

"Daniel!"

I ran up to Daniel, who slowly began standing up with the weapon in his hand. Mark fell to the floor, still laughing.

"She's a fucking whore, mate."

Daniel bent down, and pressed the pistol against his temple,

"I love her."

'He loves me. Daniel Sotherby loves me.' Through the shock, fear and unexpected confrontation with Mark, all I could focus on was that Daniel *loved me*.

Everything else seemed so far away. Distant. Like music in the background. Nothing else mattered. Nothing else made sense. There was nothing more I wanted than to replay Daniel's confession to Mark. *He loved me.*

Daniel stood up and placed the pistol on my dresser. Mark glanced over at me, and when I caught a glimpse of a kind of evil in his eyes I had never seen before, my entire body broke out into a shudder. Mark slowly closed his eyes and began gasping for air. "Is he gonna die?"

I turned to Daniel, not sure if we should be doing something to save him, or at the very least, call for an ambulance. Daniel nodded and when I turned back to Mark, he let out what I knew to be his one final breath. I stared at him. I had never seen a man die in front of me. His body relaxed and spread out on the floor, as though he had simply fallen asleep.

I placed my hands over my mouth, before Daniel walked over and held me against him. How close Daniel and I had come to be the body on that bedroom floor of my apartment. With his arms protectively around me, I felt safe. Shielded. He felt like home.

Daniel led me out into the living room after he picked up his phone from the window sill. He quickly called Damon, who in turn, contacted Jack Smith, Donny Jackson and the police. I sat in silence and when Daniel handed me a sweater, he smiled,

"I've got it all on tape. It's over. Everything's going to be okay."

I smiled back at him, before I took his hand, "You said you love me … you told Mark you love me … do you?"

Alice VL

Daniel sat down beside me, and squeezed my hand,

"I do. But, not like he thought or like you think, Ally. I do love you somewhere where there's a place for a best friend. *You.* But, I *still* want a chance with Lucy. I want to *try*, Ally."

My heart sank to my feet. Daniel didn't love me like *that.* For a moment, I let myself believe that there was a chance. There was hope. There was just that instant where I believed that I didn't miss my chance with him. And then, like pulling a rug out from under me, it was gone. I was disappointed. Hurt. I *did* miss my chance.

"We have amazing chemistry, Ally. I can't think of anything else when I'm with you. I become stupid when you're around and all I can think of is taking you and making love to you."

I nodded. Perhaps that's what it was. Maybe, I was just confusing love with lust again. Still, my heart hurt. My soul was in pain, and I didn't know how to explain it.

"There's more to life than sex, Ally. I want someone; a partner. I want more than just sex. I want love … and someone to share my life with. I want to wake up with someone who wants to wake up with me. I know you don't roll like that, Ally. I know I am not for you, like *that*. But, I want *that* ... and I so wished it could have been with you."

'*But. I do love you, Daniel. Yes. I do.*' Only, I couldn't say it out loud. '*I've missed my chance.*'

"Then, you should have that chance, Danny. You should ... and I hope you find all that love with Lucy."

'*No, I don't.*'

I didn't know what else to say. My heart was shattering right before his eyes, and he couldn't even see it. I swallowed back, desperate to contain my tears and hide the brokenness that were suddenly invading me. I didn't want Daniel's pity. I didn't want him to carry the burden of hurting me. He didn't deserve the consequences of my own demons.

I *did* miss my chance. It *was* too late, and it was all my fault. Not Daniel's. He saved my life that day, and it was time I stepped back and gave Daniel a fair chance at the life he was so desperately hunting, even if it was with Lucy.

When Damon Kingston arrived barely a minute later, he hurriedly walked up to me. There was no hiding the worry in his eyes, or the concern on his face.

"Are you alright?"

Alice VL

I DO (NOT) – ABOVE THE LAW

"I'm fine … thanks to Daniel …"

"What happened, buddy?"

"He showed up here … things just got crazy and chaotic. I don't even know really, but I have it all on tape?"

"Did you get anything to clear Mr. Bradshaw?"

"Yep, Ally got a full confession from him. He is as dirty as they get. He admitted to the drugs, the fire and even told her where he gets the drugs from."

"Great. I'll get that over to Judge Chandler right away and arrange for Mr. Bradshaw's release at once. You're going to need a lawyer … both of you are …"

He turned and stared at me,

"They'll want a statement from you both. I will submit the recording into evidence to make sure they don't arrest you both, but Monday morning first thing, I want you two in my office."

Daniel smiled before he turned to me,

"Yep. We'll be there."

When I saw Jack Smith and Donny Jackson walk in, I quickly got up to meet them.

Alice VL

"I better get out of here. See you two on Monday."

Daniel handed Damon his mobile phone before Damon turned to walk out of my apartment.

"I'll get hold of Mark's Captain at once."

When Jack Smith, Donny Jackson and the rest of the squad began collecting evidence, Daniel and I made our way into the kitchen.

"So, forensics will probably close off your apartment for a few days ..."

"I guess ... I couldn't live here anyways after this."

"You can come stay at my place for a few days?"

"Oh no, you don't have to ... I can call Bianca."

"Ally, just pack a bag and when they're done here, I'll take you home."

Home. His home. Not mine.

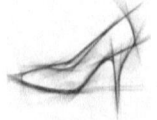

Alice VL

Mark Warren's body was removed from my apartment almost an hour later, along with his weapon and Daniel's written account of what had happened.

Once our statements were given to the detectives that were sent by Internal Affairs; my apartment was cordoned off and sealed up. After packing an overnight bag, Daniel drove me back to his apartment. We had barely walked into Daniel's apartment when my mobile phone rang,

"Michael?"

"Hey Ally …"

"You okay?"

"Yeah … we just got home. Damon Kingston just told me about what went down."

"It's over, and I am glad you and Lily have been cleared and released. I am sorry, Michael. I never intended for this to happen …"

"I am such a dick, Ally. I am sorry. For everything. I wish you nothing but the best and I swear, I'll never, ever hurt you again."

"It's okay Michael. You didn't deserve to go to jail for something you didn't do."

Alice VL

"But, you believed in me."

"That's because I know you Michael, and that's why I know you and I will never work. But, that doesn't mean I don't want you to be happy. I do. I don't *hate* you ... some of my best years were with you."

I lied. But, it didn't matter. Michael needed to hear that.

"Thanks, Ally, I get that. Lily and I are actually moving our wedding up to next month. Will you come? You can bring someone?"

"I would love to. Thanks. About a date, I am not so sure ... but let's see."

Michael was in high spirits, and for the first time in such a long time, I was at peace with him, and with Lily. Daniel at once called Lucy, and quickly told her about what had happened back at my apartment. Just as he was about to end the call, he glanced over at me, frowned, and turned back to his call, "Come over. Spend the night."

Daniel didn't trust himself around me. I didn't trust myself around him, but, I didn't want to have to look into Lucy *woozy's* face until I could get myself another apartment. Daniel

Alice VL

deserved to be happy. Daniel deserved to get what he wanted, I just wished it was me.

But it wasn't, and for the next few days, I was determined to remain strong and bravely show my support of Lucy and wish Daniel all the best.

After all, there was always Damon Kingston to distract me.

For now.

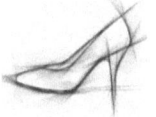

Alice VL

I DO (NOT) – ABOVE THE LAW

NOT QUITE THE END!

Mark Warren was trouble, but in all honesty, I liked the excitement and the thrill of being with him. I liked the danger and I liked the fact that he thought himself above the law. *Now, not so much.* It made me realize that safe'*ish* is just that, safe and perhaps, *better*.

I have never been one for trouble and with Mark, it was a disaster waiting to happen. Still, he was so damned sexy, smooth and rough and it appealed to me and to my physical me. But, as my encounters with Mark intensified, it was the ordinary in the extraordinary Daniel that I wanted. *Really wanted.*

Bianca was right. I was falling for him and I fell hard. But, like most things in Ally Bradshaw's life, I realized it too late and it stung. *It still stings.*

I don't know what to say? I am ashamed of the way I treated Daniel, and now that he has chosen Lucy over me, I am beginning to understand how selfish and self-serving I have become. Daniel is just the one that got away. I missed my chance with him and now Lucy gets what I initially *didn't* want. Lucy *woozy*.

Still, staying with Daniel at his apartment feels a little daunting especially since I am pretty sure Lucy will be spending more and more time over there. *She doesn't trust me.* I saw it in her eyes and I can honestly not blame her. She has every reason in the world *not* to.

I don't want to go back to my apartment. Seeing Mark's lifeless body on my bedroom floor is something I can never un-see, so I am on the hunt for a new apartment come Monday.

That is of course, after our meeting with Damon. I hope this will be resolved as painlessly as possible. After all, this is all my doing. *Yes, I know.* My sensuality's fault too. I don't much like that about me at the moment and I am hoping that my body, referred to as 'she', and I get on the same page soon.

Her wanting this and me wanting that is just not working out for either of us right now. She's a little stubborn and simply listens to nothing else but the pleasure senses she's so obsessed with.

As far as Michael and Lily are concerned, I am happy for them and am even considering attending their wedding. For now, I don't plan on taking a date with me, but who knows?

Alice VL

I DO (NOT) – ABOVE THE LAW

Both Daniel and Mark were a huge wake-up call for me, and I know that sooner or later, I am going to have to get my shit together.

Then, there's my birthday. Next Friday I turn thirty-two. *Whoop freaking whoop.* It is also my last day off before I am back at work at the museum. The arsonists still haven't been caught, so all I can do is cross my fingers and hope that lightning does not strike the same place twice.

I have no birthday plans as yet. My head is still spinning with all that went down with Mark. But, knowing Bianca, she'd probably want to go clubbing, although, there is a man in her picture. Speaking of which, I am dying to hear about her date.

I'm not sure how our living arrangements are going to play out, or how I am supposed to control myself around Daniel, but I will *try*. After all, the guy risked his life for me and I am going to do all I can to respect his feelings.

All that I can. Yeah. *Right.* Somehow, I don't quite think I am going to succeed too well.

Join me next time as I go apartment hunting, and my attempt to give Daniel the space he *thinks* he needs. Honestly, I just think he needs me, but what do I know?

Alice VL

I DO (NOT) – ABOVE THE LAW

Whatever.

I have my eye on the very fancy, very elegant and hugely attractive Damon Kingston despite my feelings for Daniel that I might add, are a pain in the ass.

My daddy always says to get back on the horse straight away, so this is me getting back on and I am hoping for a smooth ride this time.

Till next time!

Don't call me drab, boring or ugly.

Ally!

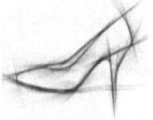

Alice VL